FALLEN

Book 2 Of The Daniel Briggs Novels

C. G. COOPER

"FALLEN"

Book 2 of the Daniel Briggs Novels
Copyright © 2015, 2018 C. G. Cooper Entertainment. All Rights Reserved
Author: C. G. Cooper
Editor: Karen Rought

GET A FREE COPY OF THE CORPS JUSTICE PREQUEL SHORT STORY, *GOD-SPEED*, JUST FOR SUBSCRIBING AT CG-COOPER.COM

DEDICATIONS

To my loyal group of *Novels Live* warriors, thanks for your
undying enthusiasm. Keep pushing me up the hill.

To our amazing troops serving all over the world, thank you
for your bravery and service.

And especially to the United States Marine Corps. Keep
taking the fight to the enemy.
Semper Fidelis

CHAPTER ONE

OLD ORCHARD BEACH, MAINE

A seagull screeched overhead as I downed the shot of Jack Daniels from a cheap plastic shot glass. The vessel matched my surroundings, suitable but far from grand. I'd arrived in Old Orchard Beach just after one o'clock in the afternoon. No real reason, other than the fact that I wanted to get off the Amtrak train and stretch my legs. Getting a few drinks and some food was a bonus, but the plan was to walk right back to the platform and keep heading north when I was done.

I asked a local where I could get a good view of the ocean, and the guy told me the best you could get was on the Pier. "But stay away from the Pier Patio Pub," the guy had said. "It's not good for tourists this time of year."

I'd ignored his second recommendation and headed straight for the Pub. The guy was right. The place was full of locals, and every head turned when I walked in and asked for a table with a view. The hostess pointed to the stairs and said I could pick any spot I wanted.

The good news was that my table did overlook the Atlantic, and the mid-May sky was fresh and clear, like someone had given it a good scrub and left me with a squeaky clean view. I love the water, always have. Along with my good friend Jack Daniels, they were the two best things I had going. Not a bad deal considering what I'd been through.

Despite being the only obvious out-of-towner in the joint, the waitress was attentive and soon brought out a bottle of Jack when I slipped her a twenty.

"You promise you'll keep track of your drinks?" she asked, not really concerned, but saying it because she had to. I imagined she was probably happy to avoid the up and down journey in exchange for a little risk.

"Scout's honor," I said, putting three fingers up in the air as I hoisted another shot in my left hand.

She looked at me funny, like she was going to change her mind about the three quarter full bottle on the table, but she smiled instead and headed back inside where I kept catching hints of French being spoken.

Must be Canadians. Tourists, I thought, gazing out over the water, wondering how cold it was and how far out I could swim. It was May. At this time of year, surely freezing, but I bet I could make it out a ways. The return trip would be a bitch, but that might not be necessary. I sat, I dreamed, and I drank. Just another day.

I sloshed the quarter remnant around in the bottle, the bitter taste of the booze long gone. As I watched the brown waves inside the square glass cage, my ears tuned in and out, like a radio receiving bits of broken traffic. The incoming news might've disturbed someone else, like someone who actually cared, but I didn't. I had my ocean and Jack Daniels. Maybe the minor annoyance would go away.

A couple minutes later, a brunette walked outside. She pretended to be looking at the view, but I saw her cool eyes wander over me more than once. She could've been looking at my messy blonde hair or my scruffy beard, but she wasn't. All legs and tight clothing, the girl was on the downswing from hot. She'd had her day for sure, but I noted the tired crow's feet highlighting her eyes, and took in the high heeled sandals that had definitely seen better days. She was like a Barbie doll cast aside after four or five years of spirited play at the hands of a toddler.

I kept swirling the bottle and refilling my plastic cup. Three drinks later, she came over.

"Do you have a light?" she asked.

I didn't look up.

"No, sorry."

That didn't change her course.

"Mind if I have a drink?"

I shrugged and handed her the bottle. She was either mustering up courage or trying to add to her new hard look because she ignored the extra plastic cups on the table and drank straight from the bottle. No flinch. No hard swallow. A pro...like me.

"Thanks," she said, handing the nearly empty bottle back. "Mind if I have a seat?"

"I'd rather you didn't," I said. "Just enjoying the view and then it's back to the train."

She stiffened just perceptibly, but then played it off by putting her hand on my shoulder. I kept swirling the bottle.

"Are you sure you don't want some company?"

I raised the bottle again, a peace offering.

"Take this, I'm done."

When I looked up there was fire in her eyes. Her pretty little nostrils flared. She stood there for a minute. I could see her thinking. *No, not a pro, a wannabe*, I thought.

Miss Past-Her-Prime stepped back and slammed the bottle onto the ground. It didn't shatter like she'd probably expected. The best she got was a split at the point where the neck met the body of the glass container. That seemed to rile her further.

"How dare you touch me!" she screamed. "I'm calling the cops!"

I sat back and looked up at her, smiling like it was exactly what I wanted.

"Be my guest. I'll be right here."

By this time, the French Canadian babble had stopped. I heard chairs scraping and then heavy footsteps like a little troupe stomping my way.

The girl grinned. "You're in trouble now."

Five guys appeared at the doorway. I'd seen them when I came in. Local meatheads, or maybe traveling meatheads. There was a tall skinny guy with his flat-billed ball cap turned sideways. Then there were the two guys who looked like twins, their necks as big as my thigh. The last two were the most drunk, sporting matching hockey jerseys, still sipping on their beers, pointing at me and whispering in each other's ears like I couldn't hear them.

"Is there a problem?" the tall guy asked the girl.

"Yeah, this guy just grabbed my ass and then said he wanted to bend me over the table."

The two drunk guys laughed and whispered some more, but the other three stepped forward.

"Hold on," I said, putting up my hands in a T like I called a timeout. "What's your name?" I asked the girl.

She made a face like she wasn't going to answer, and then said, "Tiffany."

"Tell me, Tiffany, which one of these guys bent you over a table before I came in for a quiet drink?" I was watching the meatheads, and the tall guy's eyes narrowed. "Wait, let me guess. The skinny asshole with the stupid hat, right?"

Tiffany's eyes narrowed too. "How dare you—"

"No. How dare you, Tiffany? All I wanted was a few drinks and some time to enjoy the view. Now I have to deal with your trampy ass, these guys clouding the air with their Guido cologne, and you ruining the last of my bottle."

Again, not the response she'd expected. Her eyes darted to her most recent lover, a plea for assistance.

The collective stepped closer. They were now eight feet from where I was lounging in my chair. I didn't have any weapons and, to give them a little credit, it didn't look like they did either. By the looks of the hands on the muscle-bound twins, they usually did the heavy lifting.

Mr. Tall took another step toward me as the girl moved out of the way.

"You got any money on you?" he asked.

"Some," I answered truthfully.

"How much is some?"

"Fifty seven dollars and sixty two cents."

Mr. Tall snorted. The drunk duo snickered. Thick Neck One and Two stared at me.

"You always know exactly how much you have in your pocket?" Mr. Tall asked, grinning at his friends like I was the weird one.

"Sometimes," I said. "You always hang out with the whore you're tag-teaming with the ambiguously gay duo?" I asked, pointing at the drunks. That stopped the giggling.

"You know what, I was gonna let you off with a little toll, but now I think we're gonna beat your ass and drag you down to the ATM."

I shrugged and almost went to grab for the bottle that was no longer on the table. I laughed at my slip, and for show, I half staggered to my feet. Dr. Jack Daniels had done his job, and my body was warm and calm, no shakes, just steady.

"Sorry fellas, but I've gotta catch a train," I said, reaching into my pocket so I could pay my tab.

"You're not going anywhere, asshole," said Thick Neck One.

My eyes widened in surprise. "It speaks!" Grinning like an idiot, I raised my hands in surrender. "Fine, you win. Like Tiffany over there, I'm a lover, not a fighter."

That brought back the giggles from the drunkos, and a shared look between Mr. Tall and Tiffany. Thick Neck One stepped forward. His arms lowered, his guard coming down as I staggered a bit to the left. *Bad move, Thick Neck One.*

I shifted my weight back, like I was going to stagger into the railing, but just as quickly I shifted my momentum, raised my boot, and shot it down at a forty five degree angle, every ounce of my adrenaline screaming forward. My boot caught the side of Thick Neck One's bow-legged knee. I felt the crunch, and moved to the left as he came crashing down. Mr. Tall's jaw dropped open and I took that as a perfect opportunity to close it for him, courtesy of a driving uppercut. He went up on his toes, his eyes already rolling back in his head, and then he joined his buddy on the ground. Two down, three to go.

Thick Neck Number Two actually snorted like a bull and charged, his arms wide, ready to body slam me into the wooden planks I'd served up as beds for his companions. He was close, but I waited until the last possible nanosecond. Then I dropped to my knees and punched out with both of my fists. I was hoping the guy didn't juice too much because I wanted to connect with what remained of his family jewels. Luck was with me and not with him.

He still bowled me over, but not before he'd received a double blast to his most prized possessions. His hands went to his groin as I pushed him off, rolling to my feet to face the last two. They stood there like morons, unable to make a decision as they stared at their friends on the ground.

"Who's next?" I asked.

They looked at each other like Tweedledee and Tweedle-dumb, and bolted for the door.

Then it was just me and Tiffany still standing. I ignored her and searched Mr. Tall's pockets. There was a pitiful wad of cash and a set of keys. I pocketed the cash and chucked the keys off the pier. The Thick Neck Twins at least had a few twenties each, and neither seemed to care as I stripped them of it.

Tiffany watched me do it, but didn't say anything. It wasn't until I was finished, my backpack over one shoulder, that she actually spoke.

"What are you, a ninja or something?"

There wasn't a hint of fear in her voice. She was used to being in the middle of the maelstrom.

"No, just a Marine," I said.

I stepped over Mr. Tall, who was just groaning back to consciousness, and went to pay for the bottle of Jack. From there it was either a swim out to sea or a warm shower in a cheap motel. Maybe this time I'd leave it up to a flip of a coin to decide. I didn't care either way.

CHAPTER TWO

Tails won. Instead of heading for the surf, I hit the street. I'd decided to get a room at one of the coastal hotels that catered to tourists. It was still the off-season, so I was sure to get a decent rate. I wasn't broke, but it wouldn't hurt to conserve what I had left. With just over a hundred extra bucks in my pocket from the clowns at the pub, I walked off the pier and aimed straight down Old Orchard Street.

I stopped at the first intersection and looked up at the sign telling me that the cross street was called East Grand. After looking ahead to where the train tracks crossed over Old Orchard Street half a block away, I decided to turn right, maybe skirt the coast for a bit. I wasn't necessarily in a rush to get away from the scene of the crime, but I did figure that the cheaper motels would probably be on the outskirts of the main part of the quiet town.

There was an electronics store on my left, and I debated going in to see if I could get a good GPS. The plan was to make it to Canada and see where the road or the wilderness took me. I'd need a good map or a GPS if my destiny was to go into the wilds. Again, a flip of a coin would decide the road I'd take.

I looked into the window of the store and caught the eye of the old proprietor. He glared at me and I stared back. After a few seconds, I nodded and kept walking. That guy wasn't going to be of any help, and it looked like he'd pitted his business firmly in the cheap electronic tourist trap category instead of the reliable electronic goods column.

My stomach grumbled. I should've eaten something at the pub. The food I'd seen didn't look all that appetizing, but my years of eating military rations had cured me of any food snobbery I might've had. Food was food. It got me from day to day. Half the time I didn't taste it anymore.

Up ahead was a bold blue and gold facade with a sign that said Ernesto's Dockside Restaurant. There was a beat up pickup out front with cardboard crates stacked in the back. As I approached, a guy in a priest outfit came out the front of the restaurant, or maybe it was a pastor, I could never tell. He had on one of those black shirts with the white thing in the middle of the collar. They always reminded me of my Corps dress blues with the scratchy high neck.

The priest/pastor was carrying a stack of cardboard boxes, aiming for the back of the pickup. He almost got there, but the top box tipped, and all the swaying he did couldn't stop it from falling off the stack and spilling its contents into the street.

I rushed over to help him, scooping handfuls of vegetables back into the box. He set the rest of the boxes into the truck and bent down to finish the repacking.

"I think some of this stuff is bad," I said, noticing the brown edges and the wilted leaves.

"It's okay," the man said, "They cut around the bad stuff."

Once we'd gotten the rest of the contents back in, he hoisted it into the bed with its companions.

"Thanks for your help," the man said, sticking out his hand.

I took it and nodded.

"You new around here?" he asked, not in a way that spoke down to me, just curious. He was probably in his early forties, with an easy smile that no doubt did a number on potential parishioners. The only priests and pastors I'd ever encountered were world-class salesmen. If you weren't careful, they'd have you singin' to the Lord before you could say "No, thanks."

I nodded again. "Just looking for a place to spend the night. Do you know of any cheap motels?" I don't know why I asked him. The town wasn't big and I could just as easily wander around and find a suitable place to lay my head.

He thought about it for a moment, and then said, "You just passed the Grand Victorian. It's nice, and some of the rooms have a good view of the ocean, but it's not the cheapest. Then you've got the Seabreeze just around the corner. It's clean and I know the owner. He'd take good care of you."

"Thanks for the tip."

He smiled and closed the back of the pickup as I kept walking. I heard him open and close the driver's side door and turn on the engine. It took a little effort, the whining starter complaining to the guy behind the wheel, but it finally caught and I put it out of my mind.

The motel was right where the guy said it was, and I almost took a left to cut across a parking lot to get there, but I decided to keep walking along East Grand. There was a cool breeze coming in from the ocean, and it did its best to wake me from my dulling senses. If I was going to find a place to stay, I'd need to do it soon. The alcohol coursing through my veins was singing me lullabies, and the promise of a pillow under my head almost made me turn back.

But I didn't. Instead, I forced my mind to clear, to ignore

what my body needed. Three blocks up I was again thinking about taking that swim. Maybe another flip of the coin to let fate decide.

By now I'd passed six motels, some newly renovated and some showing their age. I ignored them all and stepped to the edge of the sidewalk and pulled a quarter from my pocket.

Heads I swim and tails I keep walking.

I flipped the coin over a couple times, and was just about to toss it in the air when a pitiful honk caught my attention. Looking back the way I'd come, I saw the battered pickup of the pastor (I figured he was a pastor because he didn't talk like any priest I'd ever met), and the guy's left arm was waving to me out the window.

I clutched the quarter in my fist and waited for the truck to stop.

"I guess you decided against the Seabreeze," the guy said.

"Thought I'd keep walking, get some fresh air."

The pastor nodded, like he was concerned about my decision.

"I've got a couple deliveries to make, but if you're up for it, we've got a small guest room at our church. I wouldn't mind calling ahead and having my daughter change the sheets for you."

"I'm not one of your charity cases," I said. "I have money."

The pastor didn't look offended.

"I know that. It's just that I hate to see you have to pay for a room, dinner and breakfast. I was new to this town once, so I know what it's like to keep shelling out cash. You're just lucky you passed through in the off season."

He was trying to be nice, I could see that, but all I wanted was to be alone and to sleep. Besides, I was sure the good pastor didn't have a supply of booze at his little church. That would be a problem.

"I'm good. Thanks anyway," I said, and made to leave.

"Hey, you wouldn't be the guy that roughed up a couple of hooligans over at the Pier Patio Pub, are you?"

I turned and looked at him, saying nothing.

"Because if you are, the cops are on their way and I'm pretty sure one or more of them is about to be taken to the hospital."

"How do you know?" I asked.

"It was my last stop after seeing you. The hostess told me what happened."

I could've run or just walked away. It would be easy to disappear. That's what people didn't get. If you were halfway smart, and knew the places you should and should not go, disappearing was damn easy.

I didn't disappear. I don't know if it was the alcohol-induced calm or the sincerity in the pastor's voice, but I said, "Why would you want to help someone who did that?"

He shrugged as if he'd seen it a thousand times. Maybe he had.

"Guys like them come down from Canada all the time. They're looking for trouble and nine times out of ten they find it. Our cops don't like it, and neither do the bar owners, but it's hard to turn away business, especially when it's not peak season. Anyhow, the hostess said the guys deserved it, and I'll bet she's right."

I stared at him, looking for any sign it was some kind of trap, a ruse to get me to go to the cops. He didn't shift or look away. He just stared right back, that same funny look on his face, like a kid who didn't care what the next moment would bring.

"Could we stop at a convenience store on the way?" I asked.

"Sure."

I nodded and found myself walking around to the other side of the cab. I took off my pack, opened the door, and slid in. The interior smelled like motor oil and shoe leather. I buckled my seat belt and he put the truck in drive.

Before he released the brake, he looked over at me and extended his hand again.

"Ed Walker," he said.

I shook his hand for the second time that day, and replied, "Daniel. Daniel Briggs."

CHAPTER THREE

There were times when I didn't think the good pastor knew where the hell he was going. Inevitably, he'd make a eureka face and pulled into a driveway. Leaving the truck idling, he stepped out and grabbed a box from the back. He didn't ask for my help and I didn't offer it. After the third stop, he pulled into a convenience store where I bought a bottle of water and a handle of Jack Daniels.

Pastor Walker didn't say anything about that either, not even a sideways glance. I didn't know if he was being nice or if he just didn't care. In my half-drunken state I even wondered if he was going to take me to some place in the woods and take everything that I had. Not that I would've cared, I didn't have much on me, but even as ragged as I was, the guy was no match for me. I grunted my amusement as the pickup pulled out of the strip and back onto the main drag.

I lost count after six stops and took to staring out the window at the quaint little homes propped on well-tended lawns. It struck me as odd that the people in those homes were obviously in need, as evidenced by the second-hand food delivery, and yet, they still kept their yards tidy and their aging homes on par with the rest of the community.

After the last box left the truck bed, Pastor Walker turned the sputtering vehicle west and into the late afternoon sun. I kept yawning and almost dozed off. More homes flew by, then a golf course and next we rambled over some big interstate. I felt the truck slowing and saw an intersection coming up ahead.

Pastor Walker pointed. "That's the church up there," he said, gesturing past the intersection. It looked more like a barn than a church. You couldn't miss its rooster red roof and painted gray exterior. The place looked like something a fancy designer thought a barn should look like, all coordinated and sharp.

I didn't say what I was thinking as he took a left turn on Jenkins Road and then pulled into the first driveway on the right. There were huge bushy trees standing guard close to the house, making it hard to see what you were coming up on. When we broke past the sentinels, the size of the home surprised me. It wasn't huge, but definitely not what I expected.

The driveway looped all the way around the two-story home, and I soon saw two more buildings on the property. The one closer to the house looked like a smaller version of the big house, and the other looked like an old barn where some farmer used to stack hay.

"That's where you'll be staying," the pastor said, pointing to the small house.

The booze must've been getting to me because I almost blurted, "Are those the slaves' quarters?" Instead I said, "Looks nice."

"It's got one bedroom, a small kitchen and a full bath. No television or air conditioning, but it's cozy."

I nodded and almost groaned at the thought of a bed. My stamina waned and my body begged for rest.

Thankfully, he parked right next to the guest house. I tried not to seem too eager as I followed him through the door and listened as he gave me the dime tour. There wasn't much to the place, and it looked like most of the furniture was hand-me-downs from old ladies, but he was right, it was cozy and clean.

"There are towels and soap under the bathroom sink and the sheets on the bed are clean. Feel free to join us for dinner at seven."

"Us?" I asked.

"My daughter and me."

"You're not married?"

He shook his head.

"Is there anything else I can get you?"

I couldn't think of anything other than some privacy so I could flop down on the bed. Then I thought of something.

"I'd like to pay you for the room."

"It's really not necessary," he said.

"I insist," my mouth felt dry and I could sense that my words might be slurring. You never knew if you were the one slurring the words. *Keep it short*, I thought. "How about fifty bucks for the night?" It seemed reasonable to me and a bargain compared to what the sharks on the beach would've charged.

"Deal," he said, and turned to leave. Pastor Walker stopped at the door and looked at me. "I just want you to know that you'll be safe here, Daniel." I knew he really meant it, like those people who say, "Everything is going to be okay," but I'd been around too many shitty situations to believe him. If life had taught me anything, it was that the second you thought things were good, the universe cocked an arm and punched you right in the face.

I kept my thoughts to myself again, forced a smile, and said, "Thanks."

He returned my smile and left. I exhaled and walked into the bedroom, falling face first onto the bed. I don't remember falling asleep.

———

I WOKE to the sound of the old pickup truck starting, or at least trying to. It was giving someone a helluva time with its whining and coughing. I went to open my mouth and found my lips were stuck together from a severe lack of saliva. My tongue searched for moisture and found none. I needed water.

Turning onto my side, I saw the old fashioned clock on the side table, the kind with the two bell looking things on the top. It said six thirty-four. I searched my mind for a minute, sure that we'd arrived just after six o'clock. That's when I realized that I'd slept through the night and into the next day. It was morning.

I rubbed my face with my hands and eased off the bed. There was no hangover, just a rumble in my stomach and the nasty taste in my mouth, like onions and booze.

When I got to the bathroom, I turned on the water and put my mouth under the faucet for a good minute. Once I felt halfway awake and no longer in need of immediate hydration, I stripped down and turned on the shower. It was frigid, but that's what I needed, and it was my usual routine anyway.

I stepped into the icy water and focused on my breathing. The chill swept away the cobwebs and yanked me back to the land of the living. The water warmed gradually, and I took my time lathering up and rinsing off.

Once out, dry and dressed in the only spare set of clothing I had, I left the privacy of the guest cottage and walked toward the house. The front door was open and I could smell biscuits as I got closer. I knocked on the door-jamb. No one answered. I stepped inside and said, "Hello?" Again, no answer.

I followed the only sound in the house, what at first I thought was a radio and then realized was someone singing as I moved deeper into the house. The singing and the smell was coming from the kitchen. Now I heard the sizzling of food on a skillet, and then came the aroma of greasy bacon.

I looked inside and saw a girl with straight black hair rocking back and forth in front of the stove. She had a pair of headphones on and was oblivious to my presence. I didn't want to scare her so I said, in my best not scary voice, "Hello?"

She didn't jump, but she did turn.

"Good morning," she said cheerfully, lowering the head-phones to her neck. "Hungry?"

She must've been about fourteen or fifteen. Her eyes were a piercing blue, like a sheet of Arctic ice. The only way I could describe her face was to say that it was regal, like one of those duchesses or something. But she didn't look at me like I was some lower class schmuck. Her smile was warm and welcoming, like she was happy to see me in the most sincere way possible.

"Yeah, I'm starved," I answered finally.

"Awesome, because I made a ton," she said, turning back to the stove. "I'm Anna, by the way."

"I'm Daniel," I said reflexively.

"I know, Dad told me."

I felt a little weird being in a house alone with a teenage girl. It wasn't that I was attracted to her, but I wasn't often alone with people, and I couldn't remember the last time I'd talked to a girl, let alone a teenage one. She didn't seem to mind, though, and kept going.

"We missed you for dinner last night. You must've been tired. Dad said you came in on the train. Where did you come from?"

She talked fast, like a kid on caffeine, but not in an annoying way, more like she had a lot to say and wanted to get it out in an efficient manner.

"I came up from Florida," I answered.

"Ah, you're lucky. I've always wanted to go to Florida. Dad says he's going to take me some day. I hear the water's green down there."

"They call it the Emerald Coast on the gulf side, along the Panhandle," I said, for some reason feeling the need to explain it to her.

She nodded seriously.

"Is it true they have manatees? I love manatees. They're so cute."

I chuckled.

"I'm not sure."

I'd never seen a manatee during my time on the coast. I'd seen plenty of other things, including my fair share of the ocean, but never manatees.

"Where'd your dad go?" I asked, hoping he was close by.

"He's out back working on the truck. He's always working on the truck. I hope it didn't wake you up this morning."

"It's okay. It was better than some of the other wake-up calls I've had."

She turned and stared at me, like she was expecting me to say more. I didn't, and she turned back to the bacon.

"Breakfast will be ready in five minutes. Could you go to the back and get Dad?"

"Sure."

WE SAT down at the kitchen table and Pastor Walker said

grace. He finished it with, "And Lord, thank you for giving us this time with our new friend Daniel. Amen."

I looked up and saw Anna smiling at me and then she rolled her eyes as if to say, "My Dad always does that."

I ate in silence, making sandwiches out of the biscuits, scrambled eggs and bacon. Not Anna. Anna talked and talked. At one point I watched her, amazed that she could eat and talk at the same time. It got easier as I plowed through my first and then my second helping of breakfast. Her voice was young and inquisitive, just on the cusp of becoming an adult. And she talked very matter-of-factly, like everything was important. It might've bothered someone else, someone who thought teenagers should listen instead of speak, but it didn't bother me. Her innocence was refreshing, like encountering a person who'd never seen any of life's evils. I found myself longing to hear more, like maybe the mere sound of her voice could wash away the memories.

When breakfast was over and the dishes were cleaned and put away, Pastor Walker excused himself. "Mrs. Fendling isn't doing well. I told her I'd stop by."

Anna gave her dad a hug and kiss and then shooed him out the door. When he'd chugged down the drive and back toward town, Anna asked what my plans were.

I surprised myself by saying, "I was going to hop on a train north, but do you think your dad might let me stay another night?"

Her face lit up like I'd just told her I'd saved her father's life.

"He wouldn't mind at all. Just make yourself at home and let me know if you need anything."

I went back to the guest house and thought about climbing back into bed, this time under the covers. But instead of fading out again, I grabbed the dented metal flask with a weathered Marine Corps eagle, globe and anchor on one side, and filled it from the handle of Jack Daniels. With that task done, I pocketed the flask and headed for the door. A nice long walk would do me good.

ANNA TOLD me the land they lived on, loaned to the small congregation by a wealthy guy who owned half of Old Orchard Beach, included the three buildings and close to fifty acres of farmland.

"We haven't farmed it since we've been here, but Dad keeps talking about it."

After accepting a bottle of water and a general description of the layout of the property, I stepped into the cool morning.

I walked slowly, savoring the solitude and imagining what life would be like on a farm. No worries other than the rise and fall of the sun and tending to the land and any animals you had. I knew plenty of guys in the Corps who said they'd find a plot of land and work it after leaving the Big Green Machine. Some of those guys never made it back. I didn't know about the rest. Keeping in touch wasn't really my thing.

I skirted the edge of the property, catching glimpses of rabbits and the occasional deer through the vegetation. The land needed tending, and I decided to offer my services to the pastor. It'd been awhile since my time as the neighborhood lawn guy, but I was sure it would come back to me quickly.

As I looped around the far corner of the property, I could almost smell the presence of water. There had to be a spring or a creek nearby. Sure enough, a couple minutes later I found the brook that ran into the woods and skirted the southern edge of the Walkers' land. I followed it until the untended fields were out of view, squatting every few minutes to dip my hands in the water and turn over a rock or two. It was like when I was a kid, out hunting for crawdads and minnows with my friends.

I was halfway through the woods when something caught my eye. As I got closer, I saw that it was some kind of structure, low and dark. It was made of concrete, and tangled vines covered its sides. It was probably twenty feet by ten feet. A sad rectangle. When I stepped around to the front, I was surprised, not that there was a door to the place, but that it was cleared of woodsy debris, and there was even a window mounted AC unit above the door. It wasn't on, but I could tell it worked.

I tried the doorknob with no luck. There was a deadbolt above the doorknob and I gave it a look. It wasn't anything fancy, but served its purpose. Normally I probably would've let it be and walked on, but that morning I felt refreshed, like a part of the old me was back. My curiosity itched.

Having a military background had its advantages, one being the opportunity to pick up unique talents you'd probably never learn in the civilian world. Some could be applicable to the outside, and some might not. I never thought I'd use this one in the real world, but I fished out the small case from my pocket and ripped open the Velcro seal.

The tools were a gift from a buddy of mine in sniper school. He was from the Bronx, and always used to brag that he could break into anything with a lock. He bet the entire class he could out thieve any one of us, and wagered a bottle of Johnny Walker Black that he would win.

Five of us took him up on his challenge, which seemed almost impossible at the time. We would each have the same target, and the winning thief would be the one with the quickest in and out time. There were a couple caveats he explained after we had accepted. First, you couldn't just bust down the door. You had to be slyer than that. Second, you couldn't get caught. If you got caught, you were on your own.

Third, you had to do it blindfolded. Fourth, the target was the office of the Staff Non-Commissioned Officer In Charge (SNCOIC) of the sniper school.

The other four guys backed out after hearing the rules and the target. Not me. Something about the guy's attitude during the first half of the course bugged me. Every Marine unit had a pecking order, and this guy still hadn't figured out he wasn't at the top.

I had a week to prepare, and I spent every free minute I had learning how to break into things. Luckily, by then the Internet was already a wealth of information, and I searched for techniques and tools I could use to break in when the time came.

As we gathered for the impending mission, the challenger told us all he'd learned to pick locks from his uncle who used to bust houses for a small crime outfit (read: the Mob) in New York City. He said he wanted to go first so we could see that a) it was possible, and b) there was no way I could beat his time.

I'll give it to the guy, he was good. He never fumbled and he never cheated. He was in and out of the office in five minutes flat. When he rejoined the group, he was holding a framed picture of the SNCOIC and his wife that he'd snatched from the Gunny's desk.

"Your turn," he said to me, handing over the picture frame.

That was the night I found out I was a little bit different. It took me three minutes and thirty-seven seconds to make my silent way in and out. It gave me such a rush, and the other guys were whooping and hollering when I got back. Let's just say I got the bottle of Johnny Walker along with the tools from a very reluctant Marine sergeant.

So now I could put those skills to use. I'd done it overseas and in covert barracks raids against rival platoons, but this was my first time in the real world.

Out of habit, I counted the seconds as I worked. It took me forty-two to open the door. I was rusty.

The first thing I noticed as the metal door scraped open was the smell. It didn't smell like an abandoned shed, all dust and mildew. Instead, it smelled of disinfectant and newly washed laundry. I couldn't sense any human presence within, but my guard was definitely up. Once the glow from outside illuminated the entrance, I found a light switch and flipped it on. A row of fluorescent bulbs flickered on overhead. My chest tightened. All along the concrete walls were chains, each fastened to a secure metal hoop. On the other end of the chains were thick shackles, like something you'd see at a circus or maybe a zoo.

But this wasn't a place to keep animals. Next to each set of chains, of which I counted at least fifteen, were short wooden cots, the kind you fold and keep in the closet until guests arrive. There were sheets and blankets folded neatly at the head of each bed. Along with the cots came orange work buckets, stained brown on the inside.

I pulled the flask out of my pocket and took a healthy swig. When I was finished, I turned off the lights, reset the lock, and downed the rest of the flask. My blood felt like it was boiling, heating my flesh and burning my eyes.

Pastor Walker had some explaining to do.

CHAPTER FOUR

"Turn around, slowly," came the voice from behind. I was more pissed than concerned. People didn't usually sneak up on me. He was close, probably ten feet or less by the sound of his voice. Good and bad.

I did as instructed, even putting my hands in the air as a sign of surrender. Pastor Walker's eyes met mine. He had a shotgun in his hands that was pointed at the ground, and a bulky backpack thrown over one shoulder. More supplies for the bunker.

"What are you hiding, Pastor? Are you into some kinky stuff? Because that doesn't look like a shelter for recovering addicts." I took a step closer.

"Stay where you are." There was concern in his eyes, and by the way he held the shotgun, I knew he was no expert with the firearm. A smart guy, or someone who'd actually seen real violence, never would have dropped his muzzle. Center mass unless the other guy was on the ground, and then he'd better be dead or subdued.

"I'm unarmed, Pastor." I took another step forward. The barrel came up like it should have already. *Good boy*.

"I said don't move."

I nodded and stared at him.

"Why don't you tell me what that place is for?"

"It's none of your business."

I smiled.

"It is my business now. Do you think I'd leave without knowing what the hell is going on? Do you think I'd let you keep doing whatever you've been doing with your daughter still living with you?"

"Leave Anna out of this."

His eyes burned, but there was no conviction there. He knew he was stuck, couldn't let me go, couldn't let me run my mouth to the cops. But he didn't have the balls to do what really needed doing.

"Okay. Then shoot me," I said, taking another step closer, and even pointing at my chest. Five feet.

"I'll do it," he said, his arms starting to shake.

I shrugged.

"You wouldn't be the first to try."

His eyes scrunched in confusion. I didn't know if it was because of my comment or because he couldn't fathom my lack of personal concern. Either way, his body relaxed a bit, I saw his trigger finger waver, hesitating. I don't hesitate.

My right arm swung down diagonally, and I palmed the barrel of shotgun, easily wrenching it from his grasp. I followed that by pivoting on my left foot and delivering a crushing side kick with my right. It blasted him in the chest and he flew back and hit the ground. Before he could try to take a breath, I was on top of him, my left foot planted on his chest and the shotgun aimed at his face.

His eyes were wide as he tried to breathe, and finally the wind came back to his lungs.

"Tell me what it's for," I said.

He shook his head and there were tears running off his face.

"Tell me or I will shoot."

If this sick bastard had done anything to that sweet girl who'd made me breakfast, he deserved it. One less pervert on the streets.

"It's not what you think," he said, his voice cracking.

"So tell me."

Our eyes met and he saw that whatever compassion or lack of decisiveness he'd had was not how I was wired.

"Okay," he said.

I removed my boot from his chest and motioned for him to sit up. My aim never wavered.

"They made me do it," he said.

"Who made you do what?"

Walker looked past me at the shelter and shook his head sadly.

"It's a long story."

"I've got time," I said.

He wrapped his arms around his knees and hugged his chest to his thighs like kids do.

"I didn't have any money to start the church. I tried doing fundraisers, but everything flopped. We were living day to day on handouts from a handful of parishioners, but I knew we wouldn't last long. Then I heard about a boutique savings and loan in Boston. Their website looked promising, so I drove down for a meeting. They were pretty nice and seemed to understand my predicament. About an hour later, and after doing the necessary credit checks on me, they made me an offer. It wasn't great, the interest rate was high, but I was desperate. I knew I could make the church a success, and their faith in me seemed to prove it.

"I came back north and put the money to work. We rented a property on a month-to-month basis, nothing extravagant, just what we needed. But just like the first time, the money kept going out and none was coming in. I won't lie, I didn't know exactly what I was getting into when I spent my life savings, and all of Anna's college fund, on my dream. I really thought I could make it work. My payments to the guys in Boston got later and later. The bills were piling up and the stress of keeping everything together almost ruined me."

He stopped for a minute. I waited. He started again.

"One day a car full of guys showed up at my door. One of them was the owner of the savings and loan. He politely asked if Anna could go somewhere, so I told her to ride into town and come back in an hour. No sooner had she rounded the corner on her bike than I got pinned up against the wall, my feet dangling in the air. The nice guy I met in Boston was gone, replaced by the boss. His cultured accent disappeared too. He laid it out for me. Either I help them or else he'd kill me and take Anna."

Of course I felt for the guy, but I didn't let it show. I knew there were plenty of assholes out there willing to take advantage of innocent chumps like the pastor, but that never made it right.

"What did they want you to do?" I asked.

"He told me there was a guy who would contact me the next day. The guy was going to make a generous donation to my church."

"This land," I guessed. He nodded.

"He said I would have limited contact with the wealthy donor, and that everything regarding the land and the buildings on it would be above board, all legal. Then came the catch. He said that once we got settled in the new house, I would get a call. There would be a delivery and that I was to follow the instructions exactly or the deal was off."

Pastor Walker's eyes clouded again. He continued.

"The first call told me about the shelter and what I would do to get it ready. It took me a week to get everything I needed. Once I told them the place was ready, they sent a guy out to inspect it. All I got was a punch in the stomach as thanks, a friendly reminder of what they'd do if I messed up." He inhaled and then exhaled slowly. "The first delivery was three teenage girls, the same age Anna is now. When I got them out of the rented van, it was pretty obvious they were drugged. They always are. It's safer that way and there's no struggle." He was talking mechanically now, like he was rattling off the inner working of an automobile factory. No emotion. "I keep them here for a couple days, sometimes a week, and then I either take them close to the Canadian border where someone else takes the van, or I do the same down in Boston."

Now the pain returned to his voice and I stared at him down the length of the shotgun.

"I've thought of a thousand ways to get out of it, I really have. But it's no use. I know they'd find us."

"Why didn't you run away, disappear?" I asked. That would've been the easy solution. Hell, I did it every other day. Surely a guy as smart as he was could figure out how to live off the grid. But then I saw the weakness in him. Just like when he couldn't shoot me, he sure as hell wasn't going to run. As long as he kept up appearances and ran the scam for the Boston thugs, the pastor really thought God would deliver him from evil.

"I wanted to run, find some land out west and hide out until I knew they'd stopped looking, but I just—"

"Didn't have the balls to do it," I finished for him.

He nodded. There was no embarrassment there, only the resigned look of someone who thought the solution was no longer within reach. He'd given up, gone along with the trafficking. Well, that was about to stop.

"Please don't tell Anna," he said. "She doesn't know and I can't imagine what she'd think of me if she did."

That's when I smiled.

"I won't have to tell her, Pastor."

He looked up at me, confusion smeared on his tear-stained face.

"So you'll keep the secret?" There was actually hope in his eyes. A flicker of pity crept into my chest, but I forced it away.

"Oh no, Pastor, I'm not gonna help you keep your secret."

"But, Anna. Are you going to tell Anna?"

"Like I said, I won't have to."

Alarm in his eyes. Panic.

"But you said—"

"I won't tell her because you just did."

No sooner had the words come out of my mouth, than a shadow bolted from behind a tree, running away from our confrontation. I'd seen her as soon as the pastor told me to turn around. Anna had heard the whole thing, and all her father could do was stare at her running form in disbelieving shock.

CHAPTER FIVE

I let him get up, but grabbed his arm when he tried to run after Anna.

"I have to talk to her," he said, trying to pull away.

"You've done enough," I said.

He looked at me for a long moment and then nodded. I let go of his arm and handed back the shotgun.

"The next time you aim that thing at someone, don't let them take it away."

I could feel him staring at me as I started back toward the house. Maybe I should've walked the other way instead.

———

I IGNORED the first round of knocking. It was the pastor. I could see him from the bedroom where I was trying to take a nap and figure out my next move. It would be easy to leave. The pastor's problems weren't my problems. I'd stuck my neck out for strangers before, and the only thing I'd left was a trail of destruction.

The second round of knocking was more urgent.

"She won't open her door," Pastor Walker said.

"Then leave her alone," I said loud enough for him to hear. Silence again and my eyes closed.

The third round of knocking was more polite. I almost didn't hear it. I rolled off the bed with a groan, padded to the door and opened the door.

"What?"

He had a polite look on his face, like he was sorry to disturb me.

"She wants to talk to you," he said.

"Anna?"

He nodded.

"Look, Pastor, I understand the shit hand you've been dealt, but I don't have the time to get involved. I still say you disappear and take Anna with you. I won't say a word, I promise." The words tasted bitter as they left my mouth. Part of me wanted to help Anna, but avoidance felt like the better path.

"Please," he begged. "I'm not asking you to help. Just talk to her. I'll take you to the train station myself after you do. Just help her understand that I'm not the bad guy in all this."

My eyes must have flashed because he took a tentative step back.

"You might not be *the* bad guy in this, Pastor, but you sure as shit are *a* bad guy for going along with it. Now give me a minute to get cleaned up. I'll be over in a few, but no promises about what I'll say to her."

He nodded again, this time like a sheep doing a shepherd's bidding, and walked back to his house. I watched him go, still not knowing why I'd agreed to talk to Anna. Maybe it was the sliver of humanity I'd locked away that kept trying to get out. Maybe it was the fact that Anna fascinated me, like a rare bird you only see once in your life. Whatever it was, it kicked me back to the bathroom where I rinsed off my face,

brushed my teeth, and tried to make myself look presentable.
It wasn't much, but I figured that Anna deserved it more than
her dad.

"ANNA, DANIEL'S HERE," Pastor Walker said after knocking
on Anna's bedroom door. There was a black stenciled *ANNA*
in the middle of it, and all around it were translations of her
name. I recognized Spanish, Japanese, Arabic and even
Sanskrit.

"He can come in," she answered from behind the door. I
saw the disappointment on her father's face. Ten bucks said
he was going to try to listen. It didn't matter to me. His
eavesdropping wouldn't keep me from telling the truth.

I stepped inside, and closed the door behind me. Painted
on the walls of her room was a swirling tapestry of pinks,
grays and blacks. The Tower of London. The Leaning Tower
of Pisa. The Eiffel Tower. Then there were the ocean scenes,
beaches, dolphins and killer whales. It was like a mixture of
Van Gogh and Michelangelo, abstract meets classical. There
was even artwork on the ceiling, all centered on an ornate
crucifix with the lifeless body of Jesus hanging in the middle.

"Your work?" I asked, pointing to the cascade of color.

Anna nodded from where she was sitting on her bed. The
room was mostly bare except for the bed, a chest of drawers
and a sturdy wooden desk in the corner. The motifs on the
walls were what set the space apart.

"Impressive," I said, turning around in circles so I could
see it all. I wasn't lying. It was impressive. Another notch for
a fascinating young woman.

"Thank you," she said, scooting to the edge of the bed.
Her eyes were swollen, and her left hand held some balled
tissues.

"You okay?" I asked.

"Not really."

I nodded my understanding, not really wanting to get into the feelings of the whole thing.

"Why did you want to see me?" I asked, already planning my exit.

"I had some...questions for you." There was that curiosity in her voice again, like I'd heard in the kitchen at breakfast.

"Is it about what you heard?"

She nodded.

"I'm not sure you'll like my answers," I said. "The lying gene skipped a generation with me."

A hint of a smile appeared on her face.

"That's what I was hoping," she said. "I just...I don't understand. Why would he do something like this?"

I didn't know if she was asking it rhetorically, but I didn't have the answer to that one so I shrugged instead.

She pressed. "Why wouldn't he fight back? Why would he let those people make him do such a disgusting thing?" There were fresh tears in her eyes, a desperation to understand the breadth of the situation.

I walked over to the desk and pulled out the chair, moving it over by the bed. I sat down and looked at her.

"Some people don't fight back," I said.

"You fight back. Why can't my dad?"

"Maybe it's training. Maybe it's something you're born with. I don't know." The answer brought back memories. Marines running toward the sound of gunfire instead of away from it. SEALs rushing to the aid of a downed team member. Huey pilots flashing into a hot LZ.

"Were you trained to fight back?"

"I was."

"Who trained you?" she asked.

"The Marine Corps."

"Was it hard?"

"Sometimes."

"Did you like it?"

"Sometimes," I answered. She was starting to sound like the same girl I'd talked to before, the questions lined up and ready before I finished the last.

"Why did you get out?"

Now that was a loaded question, and one I wasn't prepared to answer. I changed the subject.

"How do you feel about what your dad said?"

That put a damper on her curiosity, but not her quick reply.

"I'm mad. Sad. More mad."

"What do *you* think he should do about it?" I asked, wondering if she'd thought it through. Something told me that she had.

"I don't know. Maybe I should call the police," she said defiantly.

"You could do that, but I'm not sure it would help."

She looked disappointed, like she'd already decided I was going to agree with her.

"What do *you* think I should do?" she asked, her gaze seeking the unspoken answer on my face.

"I think you two should leave, find a quiet place to hide for a while. It looks like travel might be one of your dreams anyway," I said, pointing again at the paintings on the walls. "Why not make it an adventure, go see things you've never seen before."

"Is that what you do? Is that why you don't have a home?"

"How do you know I don't have a home?"

She smiled. "I can just tell."

For some reason, that made me grin.

"Is there anything you don't know?" I asked, once again enjoying the back and forth.

Her smile widened and spread to her eyes. She had the

look of someone older, someone who understood things kids weren't supposed to understand.

"I don't know what *you* would do if *you* were in my dad's shoes."

I sat back and crossed my arms over my chest. She'd just asked the magic question, the one that I was not prepared to answer.

CHAPTER SIX

I closed the door quietly and left Anna to her thoughts. She wanted an answer, any answer. But what could I say? That someone should have kicked her dad's ass a long time ago? That whoever was behind the human trafficking scheme should be taken out to the woods and shot?

No, I couldn't tell her those things. Behind her facade of a mature woman still lay a little girl. She tried to hide it, painting a confident look on her face like the fancy murals on her walls, but I saw past the act. In my opinion, she was scared and that was a good thing. The pastor had gotten them in one helluva mess, and there wasn't much chance of it being fixed soon.

Pastor Walker was waiting just down the hall. I wondered if he'd listened to the conversation. It didn't really matter to me, but I was curious.

"Did you hear any of that?" I asked.

He shook his head. "I thought you'd want privacy."

I nodded and walked past him, suddenly needing food. He didn't pepper me with questions and offered me a sandwich before I could ask. Prepared in silence, the sandwich was delivered with a glass of water and questioning look from Pastor Walker.

"Is she okay?" he asked.

I took a bite of the ham sandwich before answering, using the time spent chewing to arrange my thoughts. He waited, and I took another bite, still thinking. I grabbed the glass of water and chugged the whole thing. He picked it up and went to the sink to refill it. I attacked my food, weighing the pros and cons of saying anything at all. I didn't want to get involved. A few miles down the road, the train tracks beckoned. I could already feel the familiar call of the road, like an unseen magnet yanking me forward.

I finished my sandwich and the second glass of water before speaking.

"She's mad, and she has every right to be."

"I know," he said solemnly, folding his hands in his lap.

"She says she thinks she should call the police."

There was a brief look of alarm on his face, but he replaced it with what I was coming to recognize as his "church face," the soothing look he probably gave parishioners when they came to him for help.

"I can understand why she would feel that way."

His tone almost made me slam my fist down on the table. I leveled him with a hot glare.

"You seem pretty calm considering what you're up against," I said, the words cold and accusing.

"I've made my peace with it," he said. "If God wants me to be delivered, he will show me the way."

I bolted out of my chair, sending it skittering back.

"*This* is what's wrong with you people," I said, my index finger stabbing in his direction. "You look to God for all the answers, when really you should be looking in the fucking mirror. When did God ever say that you should throw your hands up and wait to be led to water? You're a hypocrite,

Pastor! If I were you, I'd fess up to what you've done and beg your daughter for forgiveness. I'm not saying she'll give it to you, because you've probably royally fucked that up, but at least then you'd be taking some goddamn responsibility for your actions."

I was fuming. My chest expanded, the animal within me growling for release.

"Is that what you've done, taken responsibility for your actions?"

That did it. Something inside me snapped. Through the haze, I saw the kitchen table flip to the side and suddenly I had the smug bastard pinned against the wall.

"You have no idea what I've been through," I growled. "It makes your little adventure seem like a unicorn fairy tale."

The "church face" was gone, replaced by horror. He saw the beast in my eyes, and I barely controlled the rage that could easily rip him to pieces.

"Please let him go."

My breath caught. It was Anna. Somehow she'd surprised me and snuck into the kitchen in the midst of my tirade.

"Please, Daniel, let him go." Her voice was soft, but not pleading. It was more matter-of-fact, like a friend asking for a simple favor. I let go of the front of the pastor's shirt and backed away. I met her eyes. There was determination there. She was in charge now. Anna touched my arm, gave me little smile, and then walked to her father. "You need to fix this, Dad."

He reached for her, but she pushed his hand away. His face paled.

"I don't know how to fix it, honey. If I did—"

"You don't have a choice anymore," she said. "Either you fix it, or I leave."

Pastor Walker looked like he was going to collapse. His knees shook and his chest heaved. Then he took a shaky breath and said, "I'll fix it." There was only a sliver of conviction in his eyes, but he must have seen something in hers because he then said, "I promise I'll fix it, Anna."

She didn't say a word, only nodding before she headed back upstairs. I heard her door close as Pastor Walker slumped back down in his chair. He stared at the ground, not saying a word.

I thought about picking up the kitchen table and maybe cleaning things up, for Anna. Then I changed my mind, grabbed a slice of ham from the kitchen counter, and walked back to the guest house.

————

ANNA MADE us fried chicken that night. She delivered it in a wicker basket, like the ones you take on an old fashioned picnic. It was just the two of us, digging in hungrily and occasionally licking the salty grease off our fingers. For the first time since I'd met her, Anna didn't speak. I figured she had enough to think about, so I focused on the food.

I'd spent the rest of the day sleeping, and at some point I heard the rumble of the pastor's truck easing away from the main house. I wondered where he'd gone, but didn't think it was the right time to ask. Not that I really cared anyway.

Anna finally spoke. "If I leave, where do you think I should go?"

I took a minute to think about it, devouring another drumstick in the process.

"Up to you," I said.

"Could I come with you?"

I stopped eating.

"I'm not sure that's a good idea."

Her eyes went back to her food. I could see she was disappointed. A couple minutes later, she asked, "Why isn't it a good idea?"

I didn't want to tell her, and yet, I found myself answering.

"If there's trouble around, I'm usually in the middle of it. Not the best place for someone like you."

"What kind of trouble?" she asked.

I shrugged, not really wanting to explain. She stared at me until I answered.

"Fights, that kind of thing."

"Have you ever killed anyone?"

Every time I thought she was going one way, she bobbed in the opposite direction. I nodded and grabbed a juicy thigh from the basket.

"Is that why you're alone? Do you feel bad about killing people?" she asked.

I shook my head slowly. She didn't press.

"Where did you learn to cook?" I asked, veering away from the taboo thoughts that always found me in nightmares.

She smiled and said, "A couple years ago, there was an old lady, Mrs. Massey, who I used to visit. I'd stop in to check on her, and pretty soon she started teaching me how to cook. She was from Alabama and knew how to prepare every Southern dish I'd ever heard of. In exchange for my visits, she taught me what she knew. Mrs. Massey was a good friend."

By her tone I understood that the old Southern lady was dead.

"What's your favorite thing to make?" I asked.

Her face brightened. "Oh, that's easy. Bread pudding."

She went on to tell me how Mrs. Massey liked to mix in walnuts but that she preferred chocolate chips. From there she explained the difference between regular tomatoes and fried green tomatoes, and how fried green tomatoes were much better on BLTs. I finished my meal and was more than happy to sit back and listen. But as I watched her get more and more animated with her retelling, my mind half-faded away, going back to her original question from earlier in the day. *What would I do if I were in her father's shoes?*

I grinned as the answer came to me in a flash. *I would find whoever was behind the trafficking, and kill them all.*

CHAPTER SEVEN

I sat in bed after dinner, sipping on a glass of Jack, replaying the day in my head. Two sides of a coin. One half with Anna's face and the other with her father's. I flipped it over and over again in my head, marveling at the way Anna's face caught the light and the pastor's sucked in the shadow.

The sound of the pastor's sputtering truck broke my trance and I walked to the window. He got out slowly, heaving two bags of groceries from the passenger side seat. My lights were off so it was impossible for him to see me through the gloom. But I saw him look my way, a lingering gaze that looked pitiful in the dim light. His eyes were swollen and his nose was red. He kept sniffing like he'd been crying, but he finally turned away and went to the main house.

I stayed at the window, watching as one by one, the lights turned on downstairs. Anna's bedroom light was still on upstairs, and I didn't see any flickers to indicate that she'd gone to greet him. *Good girl*, I thought. *Let him stew in his self-pity*.

Anna had told me at dinner that the good pastor was off

tending to his meager following. There were always people to help and never enough food or time. I'd asked if he spent most nights away, and she said only during the week.

"Other than Sunday service, we always spend the weekends together," she'd said, softer than before.

There'd been sadness in her voice, peppered with a dose of regret, like she was having to grow up again. Her life had changed.

I downed the rest of my drink and went through my normal bedtime routine. All I could think about was that coin, and which way it would land in the morning.

———

MORNING CAME with a soft knock at the door. It was Anna, and when I opened the door, the smell of fresh-baked blueberry muffins made my stomach grumble.

"Hungry?" she asked, holding up the same basket she'd used to transport the fried chicken the night before.

I nodded and let her in. She brought an old-fashioned glass jar with fresh-squeezed orange juice and a green thermos with coffee. I hadn't slept well, and the thought of caffeine sounded good.

Anna was quiet as she set the table by laying the basket in the middle and producing two plastic glasses from her coat pocket. She nibbled at a muffin as I devoured one and then a second. I drank my coffee black, but it still tasted creamy and rich. Pouring myself a second mug, I finally asked, "How did you sleep?"

She shrugged and kept at the muffin.

"Did you talk to your dad?"

Anna shook her head.

"Are you going to talk to me?"

A little smile tugged at the corners of her mouth.

"I'm sorry. It's just that, well, I didn't sleep very well last night," she said.

"That makes two of us," I said, holding up the cup of coffee and taking a sip.

"Why didn't you sleep?"

"I don't sleep well most nights."

"Does the alcohol help?"

There was zero accusation in her tone, just curiosity again.

"Sometimes," I answered, honestly. "It helps get me to sleep, at least."

She nodded and I could see her filing the fact away.

"Are you leaving today?" she asked.

She really had a knack for getting right to the core.

"I thought I'd hang around another day, maybe help with the mowing."

Her eyes perked up at that.

"I could show you," she said, putting the muffin on the table.

"You know how to use the tractor?"

She grinned like she was hiding a secret.

"Better than my dad," she said.

I beamed back. It was hard not to. Her spirit was infectious.

"Okay, let's finish breakfast and then you can show me what to do."

ANNA FETCHED me a set of her dad's work clothes after breakfast. They were a little small in the sleeves and the legs, but there was plenty of room to move otherwise. With the precise instruction of a small-arms instructor, Anna walked me through how to check, start and run the tractor.

"It pulls to the left a little, so be careful when you're close to the creek. Dad almost put it in the water when we first moved in."

She explained the boundaries and that there were ten acres plus or minus a little that the pastor was obligated to tend.

"I do it most weeks," she said, like it was the most natural thing in the world for a fifteen year old girl to work the fields.

"Don't you go to school?" I asked.

"I do it all by correspondence," she said, "On the computer."

"Not even home school?"

She laughed. "Dad tried to teach me when I was thirteen until he realized that I picked up math quicker than he did. After that, he bought me a computer and we found a school where I could do the work at my own pace. I'm actually graduating from high school this summer."

Yet another reason to admire the girl. If I'd tried anything like that when I was fifteen I probably would've ended up in jail.

I climbed up on the tractor and asked, "Planning on going to college?"

Her smile disappeared. "I'm not sure...now."

I didn't push. There'd be plenty of time to think as I cut.

SOMETHING ABOUT MOVING up and down the pastor's land, the steady running of the engine, and the cool spring air soothed me into a rhythm. My thoughts wandered. I chuckled as I remember the movie *Forrest Gump*, and how I'd wondered as a kid why a millionaire would cut grass for free. Now I understood. It was the outdoors and the tranquil monotony of the task. I wondered if that's the way those Japanese monks felt raking their sand gardens. Maybe that's how you found your Zen.

Occasionally, my mind would flutter back to the problems at hand, to the pastor and Anna. I could just flip my coin again, random fate telling me which way to turn. And yet, the gentle rocking of the tractor beckoned me to stay, like an old horse clopping down a worn path, extending the ride as long as it could.

Anna came out to the fields at lunch and brought me leftover fried chicken and lemonade. She didn't stay, but told me that she'd be making BLTs for dinner.

"Have you talked to your dad yet?" I asked.

She shook her head and walked away. Anna was holding the line. I wondered what Pastor Walker was thinking.

After I finished up lunch, I got back on my trusty steed. Three hours later, I was done. I pulled the tractor back into its spot and turned off the engine. I felt good, like I'd just taken a dip in a cool spring and come out refreshed even though my back was slick with sweat.

That feeling dried up as soon as I turned around. Pastor Walker was standing there with an uneasy look on his face. I stepped the other way, toward the guest house.

"Wait," he said, reaching out an arm even though I was twenty feet away.

I stopped, still facing the opposite direction.

"What?" I asked, the familiar twist in my gut knotting up inside me.

"I got a call."

I turned to face him.

"And?"

His eyes were glazed and shifting.

"There's another shipment," he said.

I didn't say a word.

"I need your help," the pastor said in a lower voice.

"It's not my job, Pastor."

"What if I told you that this was the last time, that I'm

taking Anna away after this? Would you help me then?" Desperation raised dots of sweat on his forehead and his hands were shaking. He looked like a toddler could push him over.

"What do you want me to do?" I asked, the thought of Anna getting away from this situation pulling me in.

"Help me figure out how to leave."

It wasn't what I'd expected him to ask.

"Okay."

"Does that mean you'll help?" His eyes lit up like I'd just promised to deliver him from the devil.

"If it means your daughter is safe, then yes, I'll help you leave."

"Thank you so much, Daniel. I don't know how—"

I cut him off with a glare. He got the point.

"When do you pick up the shipment?" I asked.

"Tonight," he said quickly.

"Good," I said. "I can't wait to get you out of my sight."

CHAPTER EIGHT

Anna and I shared dinner in the guest house again. Pastor Walker was gone, and all I could think about was what he was doing. He'd gotten someone, probably an unsuspecting parishioner, to drop him off at the pickup point. I pressed Walker on where the location was, but he wouldn't budge. There'd been the opportunity to follow him, an idea that easily found a hold in my subconscious, and then I thought of Anna. Something told me to stay close to her, so I did.

I picked at my food as Anna chatted about her favorite places in Italy.

"I mean, I've never been there, but I'm pretty sure Rome and Venice would be my favorites. A lady I met in town told me not to go to Venice in the summer, you know, because of the smell from the canals, but she said it was really nice in the fall."

She went on, seemingly unconcerned by the lack of words coming from my side of the table. Apparently I did a decent job of bobbing my head every once in a while, and keeping the concern from my eyes.

But even as I listened, my mind flew at the speed of a computer processor. Whether I liked it or not, I was now part of the pastor's "situation." What I decided to do next would determine the swamp's depth when I stepped in. The way I figured, I had three options.

First, I could still leave. It was only an option because other people in my spot might consider it an option. I'd discarded it the moment I said I would help them.

My second option was to call the cops and see what happened. But I was a stranger in town. They might just take the pastor's word over mine and possibly throw Anna in a foster home. No, I couldn't do that. It was too risky. Calling in the authorities always carried too many potential pitfalls.

Third, I could wait. I'd spent a lot of time waiting over the years. Marine snipers are excellent at waiting. It's what we are trained for. My professional ancestors like Gunnery Sergeant Carlos Hathcock had waited days just for a glimpse of a high value target in Vietnam. I'd never had to wait that long, but there were plenty of ways to make a day-long hide miserable. Rain, heat, bugs, rats, a case of Montezuma's revenge... You never knew what would hit you until it actually happened. That's how I felt now. There were so many unknown variables that my brain kept jumping from one to another.

What if some of the thugs came back with the pastor?

What if the pastor got nabbed on the way back?

What if...what if...what if...?

It was just past seven and Pastor Walker said he'd be back around midnight. As the minutes ticked by, Anna happily recited her already-mapped trip through Europe, and I kept smiling and eating. Underneath the facade, my inner self was preparing. No matter the circumstance, I would be ready.

———

I SNUCK out of the guest house just after 11pm. Anna's bedroom light was already out, so that was one thing I wouldn't have to worry about.

Pastor Walker told me he always came in from a side entrance that meandered into the woods and dumped out near the shelter. I picked my way there, grabbing an ancient rusty sledge hammer as I passed the storage shed. It wasn't much, but it was something.

I tucked myself into a small tangle of bushes that afforded me a good view of every avenue of approach except for the one I'd taken before, which came up the back side of the building. That was the roughest path, so I'd demoted that one to the least likely on the list should more company show.

Midnight slipped by and still there was no sign of the pastor. An owl hooted in the distance, answered a few seconds later by a companion. Otherwise the night was quiet except for the swaying branches that knocked together overhead. I would've preferred a little more ambient noise, a little extra cover for my movement, but at least I'd probably be able to hear if someone drove up to the house.

Fifteen minutes later, I was still waiting. In the recesses of my paranoid self, I wondered if the pastor had lied. Maybe it was all a diversion, a way to get me away from the house and alone. If they surrounded me, that could be a problem.

But even as I began to think about what I would do if I did get cornered, I caught the sound of crunching gravel in the distance. A few seconds later, slivers of light from high beams shone through the night and soon grew brighter.

The vehicle was moving slowly, the pastor probably trying to avoid collisions on either side. I'd checked out that particular path on the way in and there wasn't much room to maneuver, especially if he was driving the usual delivery van.

A van came into view soon after, the front seat invisible behind the blinding beams of light shining my way. I waited, watching as the gray panel van stopped and the engine clunked off. When the driver's side door opened, the overhead cabin lamp illuminated Pastor Walker's face.

He got out and moved around to the back of the vehicle, keys clinking as he moved. I heard a key going into the lock, and then the two back doors opened. The doors blocked my view, but a moment later I saw bare legs ease down from the van. I counted, *One, two, three, four, five.*

The doors shut and I got my first glimpse of the five girls in the scattered moonlight. None of them ran and none of them struggled. They stood in the same spot until Pastor Walker ushered them toward the shelter.

I didn't want to take a closer look. I was too afraid of what I might do to the good pastor if I laid eyes on the girls up close. They couldn't have been older than eighteen, and all had similar straight hair and slight builds that seemed more Eastern European than American. *Ukrainian*, I thought, remembering an article I'd read out of a discarded newspaper that documented the increased human slave trade coming out of the former Soviet puppet. With the Russians once again dipping their fingers into Ukraine's well, who knew what kinds of atrocities were going on unnoticed.

The minutes ticked by again, the image of the spinning coin dancing in my head and I waited. Somehow, every time it landed on some unseen surface, Anna's smiling image always came up instead of her father's "church face."

Finally, the lights in the shelter clicked off, and Pastor Walker came out, locking the door behind him. I eased myself up as Walker finished his duties and moved to the van. He jumped when I melted into view.

"Jesus, you scared me," he said, clutching his chest like I'd shot him with an arrow.

"How did it go?" I asked, allowing the bitterness to slither into my voice.

"Fine," he said, fumbling to lock the van door.

"And the girls?"

"They're sleeping," he said, avoiding my glare.

"Drugged?"

He nodded.

"Did you give them something too?" I asked.

"It's always the same. I don't know what it is, but it doesn't take long."

"Pills or injections?"

"Pills."

"How long will they be out?"

"Until morning," he said without hesitating. I wondered how many times he'd gone through this routine.

"Okay, we'll come back at sunup," I said, turning to leave.

"Have you decided what we should do?" he asked.

I kept walking, but whispered more to myself than to him, "Not yet."

CHAPTER NINE

I jolted upright at the sound of *Snake Eyes! Snake Eyes!* still ringing in my head. My eardrums hummed like I'd just been in the middle of a firefight. Heart racing, I ran a forearm over my brow and it came back dripping sweat. That's when I realized the rest of my body was soaked too. There was no way I was getting back to sleep, and it wasn't even five in the morning yet.

Easing myself out of bed, I went to the bathroom and turned on the shower. My glance at the mirror was a mistake. My eyes were bloodshot, my beard scruffy and my hair was a tangled mess. It happened every so often, noticing what I'd become. Sometimes I thought about what others saw, but mostly I didn't care. It wasn't my problem.

Anna had not once looked at me disapprovingly. If there was a judging bone in her body, I hadn't seen it yet. As I stepped into the steaming shower, I thought about what it must be like to live life as if in a fantasy. I was running away from dreams while Anna was running toward them. What would she think if she could really see inside my head?

I let the stinging water pelt me with angry volleys, relishing the pain that came from the overpowered water pressure. My skin was tingling and red as I toweled off ten minutes later, my mind clicking on as I thought about what would soon transpire. Anna didn't know about the late night pickup, and I sure as hell didn't want her to find out. As stupid as her dad was, I knew he didn't either. The only thing he had going for him was that he loved his daughter and wanted to protect her from his choices.

I slipped into the clothes that were laid neatly on the rocking chair across from the bed. Anna could've run her own bed-and-breakfast if she wanted, her customer service skills far exceeding what I was used to. My shirt smelled like flowery dryer sheets as I put it on, and my well-worn pants were pressed for the first time in ages. The last time I'd worn anything ironed had been in the Corps, before they'd changed us over to those digi-cammies. I still missed the highly starched utilities and hyper-shined boots that I'd first seen adorning Gunnery Sergeant Thomas Highway in *Heartbreak Ridge*. To me, that was the way a Marine was supposed to look. I remembered some Drill Instructor calling that "A.J. Squared Away."

"Poster Boy Marine." That's what they'd called me. Despite my fresh laundered and pressed clothes, I was a long way from that now.

PASTOR WALKER WAS WAITING when I stepped outside. He asked if I wanted a cup of coffee. I shook my head and instead took the same path we'd returned on hours earlier. I wasn't in the mood to talk, and luckily the pastor got that. He walked a few feet behind me, one of those collapsible coolers strung over his shoulder. I assumed it was food for the girls.

How thoughtful, I mused bitterly.

The van was right where he'd left it, and there was no light coming from the shelter. It was still gray out with the occasional shaft of sunlight poking in through the vegetation. Everything was quiet again except for the crunch of our footsteps over composting leaves.

The first sign of trouble was the blanket on the ground. It was hard to see until I got closer, but once I did, my eyes traveled to the door and then to where the lock was supposed to be. It wasn't there.

"Shit," I said, pulling the door open and flicking on the lights. The place was empty except for five mussed cots. I took another step in and looked around. There was no sign of forced entry. The hair on the back of my neck was already standing, but it froze when I turned to talk to the pastor.

He was holding a piece of pink paper that I must've missed when I yanked the door open. I now saw the scrap of duct tape that had held the note on the back of the door. My heart thudded as I recognized the handwriting on the back with the words "Daddy" written on it.

Anna.

Pastor Walker looked like he'd seen a ghost as his eyes scanned the page. I ripped the paper from his hands and read it.

Daddy, What you're doing is wrong. I've prayed about this a lot, and I'm going to help you now. These girls deserve to be saved, and I'm going to do it. I'll call you when we're safe. In the meantime, pray that God will forgive you. I will do the same.

Love,
Anna

P.S. Leave Daniel out of this. He's already been through enough. Tell him I'm sorry.

———

ANNA TRIED to hurry the five girls along as best as she could. She knew they probably had a couple hours head start on her dad, and only hoped they could make it before they were either seen by the police, or caught by her father.

She'd spent the previous night thinking about things, and it was only by luck that she'd been gazing out the window when her father and Daniel returned. She had waited for the sounds from her father's room to die down, and then she'd snuck out of the house.

The shelter had been right where she remembered, only now there was a van out front. She knew there were people inside, but there was no way to get to them. At first Anna thought about using a rock or a sledge hammer from back at the house to bust the lock off, but she figured that doing so would either wake the prisoners inside or alert Daniel and her father. Probably both.

So she'd done the only thing she could think of, and went looking for keys.

She started in her father's office. As usual, it was a mess, and there were plenty of places to hide the keys, but she knew about the safe she wasn't supposed to know about. She also knew the combination. It helped to be observant with a father who was typically so scatterbrained he couldn't remember passwords or where he'd left his wallet.

Anna held her breath as she turned the soundless knob from left to right, finally clicking the safe open. And there they'd been, sitting on top of an assortment of official church files. She grabbed the ring of keys.

Shaking with excitement, she'd run back to the shelter

and unlocked it. She left it on the door, and rushed the keys back to their original hiding spot. Before returning to the woods, Anna stuffed her backpack full of food and water bottles. Then, on her third trip into the treeline, she had a thought. She needed help and almost turned to wake Daniel.

No, she thought. *He doesn't need more trouble.* This was her family's problem and she didn't want the Marine to get dragged in further.

So she'd pulled her phone out of her pocket and made a call. The person on the other end hadn't been happy to hear from her at first, but after explaining the situation, she'd agreed to help. And that's where Anna and the five girls were headed now, to a lonely stretch of road a couple miles from the farm. It was hard going since they had to stay off the roads, and it didn't help that the girls were kind of out of it, like they were on heavy painkillers or something, but Anna pressed on. She made them hold hands, and that seemed to help.

The sun was just coming up when she saw the road. Since none of the girls with vacant eyes seemed to understand English, she motioned for them to stay put. Anna ran up ahead and confirmed that they were at the right intersection. She smiled and returned to the freed prisoners.

Handing out water and snacks to the skinny girls, Anna prayed she'd made the right choice. Right or wrong, she knew something had to be done. What had finally made her act alone was putting herself in those girls' shoes, imagining the harrowing ordeal they had been through. She'd done the research online and knew that the young girls with doe eyes would either end up dead or as someone's sex slave.

Anna had seen enough deprivation in her short life that she understood better than her peers how ugly the world could be. While other teens were busy going to the mall or deciding what to wear on Friday night, Anna saw the world for what it was: a place with enormous potential, with its share of evil and heartbreak. She studied it with an eye for improvement, like a painter who was never satisfied with his work. This was her way of fighting back, of unleashing a tiny golden ray back into the darkness, and staking her claim for what was right.

CHAPTER TEN

I scanned the area with a flashlight and found the path Anna and the girls had taken. It was impossible to be accurate about how old the tracks were, but I was betting on the worst case scenario.

"She may have a two to three hour head start," I said, getting a general feel for the direction they'd headed. "Do you have a map?"

"There's one in the van," Walker said. He fetched it without having to be told. We were both on the same team now, and his grim visage told me he was at least as determined as I was to get Anna back.

I unfolded the street map and told Walker to pull out his phone and check the GPS. After a quick perusal, and judging by the meager path, I guessed they'd gone either northwest or straight west. There were intersections at each point, and by car it would be easier. If we left soon, we had a slim chance of getting there in time.

"How well could the girls travel?" I asked.

Walker shrugged. "Whatever's in the pills keeps them doped up, but doesn't seem to impede their basic senses. It's more like their bodies work but their higher brain functions are impaired."

That was good for Anna and bad for us. It meant she could make good time if she knew the way and kept the girls moving.

"I'll take the van and you get your truck," I said, grabbing the keys from Walker and sliding into the cab. But when I turned the ignition nothing happened. I tried again. Nothing.

Anna, I thought, shaking my head in admiration despite the dire consequences of her well-intended actions. She'd thought of everything.

When I popped the hood my fears were confirmed. She'd cut through hoses and belts, probably with a knife from her beloved kitchen. I smiled. The warrior in me was used to battling armed enemies. Anna was proving that a girl with a brain might easily outfox a Marine sniper.

"Let's get to the truck," I said, slamming the van door. "Hopefully she didn't sabotage that one too."

———

THE TEXT WAS short and made Anna smile.

Be there soon.

She rubbed her hands together to ward off the morning chill. The cold plus the cuts and scrapes from their journey were a small price to pay. Soon she and the girls would be safe; she'd been promised as much. Anna shivered, but gritted her teeth as she looked at the poor girls she'd rescued. They were worth the risk.

———

LUCKILY, the truck's ignition did work. It took Pastor Walker a minute to get it going, but at least it was running.

"Let's take this road first," I said, pointing to Flag Pond Road, which was just around the corner.

The engine groaned as he eased us down the driveway and out to the road.

"Do you think she's okay?" Walker asked, keeping his eyes on the road ahead, pedal depressed as far as he dared.

"She's a smart girl," I said, as if that was enough. I didn't want to talk about what could happen. There were too many variables to think about, too many what ifs.

What if a neighbor saw them and called the police?

What if one or more of the slave girls turned on Anna?

What if someone was helping them and that person turned on Anna?

"If she called someone for help, who do you think she'd call?" I asked.

"I don't know. I guess she could call someone from our congregation, but I can't think of anyone who would be of any real help. Most of them are old or completely ordinary. Anna would know that."

I agreed with his assessment and could've kicked myself for not acting sooner. She'd asked for my help, and when I didn't give it to her, she'd felt compelled to act on her own. Regret was a powerful drug, and I was getting a double dose at the moment.

We cruised along as fast as the little truck would go. When I glanced at the RPMs, I saw that we were dangerously close to the reds, even though the truck was speeding at a fraction of what any decent car could go.

I scanned the roadside as it flew by. Other than trees and the occasional house, there wasn't much to look at. We came upon the first major intersection and I ordered Walker to slow down. My eyes looked over one tree line and then another. I did three passes, just in case, but there was no sign of movement or the telltale flicker of the color of clothing.

"Let's go to the next one," I said, the dread in my stomach growing. Something told me it was too late.

———

As promised, the two vehicles pulled off the road and onto the mottled grass. Like she'd been told over the phone, there was one of those fancy Mercedes passenger vans and a Lincoln Town Car. Anna swallowed her nervousness and motioned for the girls to get up. She had the distinct feeling this was the moment where everything would change. It was impossible for her to understand how much.

———

There were red tail lights up ahead and I screamed for Walker to go faster. The pickup sputtered down the road at its pathetic top speed of just over fifty miles per hour.

I could make out forms now, and they were all getting into the vehicles. My eyes strained to see that far, and that's when I saw Anna's slender form duck into the black car.

We were probably two hundred yards away when the taillights flickered and started moving.

One hundred yards.

Now I could see two heads in the Lincoln Town Car.

Fifty yards.

They must have seen us because I detected an increase in speed on their end. The convoy matched our speed and then went faster.

Twenty yards.

One of the heads turned, and I saw the beautiful face of another woman. She smiled at us, lifted her hand, and gave us the middle finger.

My eyes went wide as I heard the clunk followed by a loud hiss.

Pastor Walker didn't seem to notice and still had the pedal stuck to the floor. Steam and smoke rose from the hood, obscuring our view of the fading automobiles. Walker slammed on the breaks and we jolted to a stop. I braced myself against the dash and turned.

"Who the hell was that?" I asked, pointing to where the Town Car had just been.

Pastor Walker's chin dropped to his chest and he said, "That's Anna's mother, my ex-wife."

CHAPTER ELEVEN

Anna kept stealing glances at her mother. She couldn't help it. They'd been apart since her parents had separated, and Anna couldn't remember a vivid image no matter how hard she'd tried. She had the fuzzy memories of muffled arguments and breaking glass, but she never knew what was real and what was just her childhood imagination. Her father never liked to talk about her mother, so for years they'd pretended it was just the two of them.

That hadn't deterred Anna from looking. One dreary morning while her father paced back and forth in his room overhead, a ritual before Sunday sermons, Anna had found a faded picture of her mother tucked away in the back of a desk drawer.

And now here she was, more beautiful than in the sun-smeared photograph from her father's desk. Her hair matched Anna's, long and dark. But where Anna's face was clean of all but the faintest wisp of lip gloss, her mother looked liked she'd just stepped off a New York runway. She even had the air of some high up CEO's wife, like she'd been bred to bathe in money.

And to think that she'd come up from Boston at a second's notice. One phone call was all it took. The thought filled Anna with regret, thinking of all the nights she'd stared at the piece of notebook paper with her mother's phone number. She'd stolen that from her father too. While she felt bad about it before, now she only felt relief. Her mother was there and she said she would help.

It was almost too much for Anna to handle, and she clasped her hands in her lap to keep them from shaking. The early morning ordeal threatened to burst the excitement out of her body in the form of endless questions and a flood of tears. Anna bit it all back, wanting to put on an adult face for her mother, the elegant Natasha Varushkin.

I GRIPPED the door handle to keep from punching Anna's father.

"You have exactly one minute to tell me about your ex-wife." I stared at my knees instead of making eye contact with him.

His answer came out slowly despite the viper sitting next to him.

"Natasha was here on a student visa when we met in Boston. I fell in love with her the moment I saw her. She was cultured and well-traveled while I was just a small town kid. I was overmatched from the start. Natasha got pregnant six months after the wedding, and for a while after Anna was born we tried to make it work. I plunged into the party scene with her and we had some good times. But then one morning, when I was reaching into the fridge for something to combat my hangover, I looked over and saw Anna in a playpen staring up at me. I'll never forget that look. She was barely eighteen months old, and yet she looked at me like an adult. It wasn't until I walked over that I noticed she was covered in her own poop. Apparently Natasha and I had forgotten to change her the night before, and it was almost noon. Something in me broke. I picked her up and held her for a long time. I cried and she just kept her head on my chest. I don't know how long we sat like that.

"Once Natasha woke up, I told her what had happened and suggested we make a change, maybe move out of the city. She laughed at me and said I was welcome to take Anna and leave. I really thought she was kidding, or maybe that she was still drunk, but her tone never changed, not that day, not the next week. We fought and I pleaded. Natasha just kept partying and some nights never came home. So I did what I had to do. I took Anna to a friend's and filed for divorce the next day. The papers came back quickly, and Natasha never asked to see Anna again. That was over thirteen years ago."

We sat in silence for a long moment. What do you say to that? Sure, I felt for the guy, and he'd done the brave thing back then, but why hadn't he followed through?

"How did Anna contact her mother?" I asked.

"She must have found the phone number in my office. I kept it in case of emergencies. I thought I'd hidden it, but..."

I actually laughed a little. Anna had already shown that she had ample intellect to outsmart her father. In the span of less than a day, the teenager had managed to steal from her father's safe, release five prisoners, disable a vehicle, and contact her mother who she hadn't seen in over a decade. The girl would either make a perfect criminal or a talented operative if given the chance.

"Your ex still lives in Boston?"

"She does."

My next question was cut off by flashing lights and gentle

honk behind us. I turned and saw a tow truck pulling up to our right.

"Someone you know?" I asked.

Pastor Walker nodded, and then shook his head like he was casting off invisible cobwebs. When he looked up he had the "church face" on again. He almost looked normal. I rolled down the window as the face of an overweight driver came into view.

"Having trouble with your truck again, Pastor?"

The guy looked like he would've been more at home south of the Mason-Dixon, playing the part perfectly with a heaping mound of chew in his cheek. He spat a glob onto the pavement.

"Good morning, Melvin," the pastor greeted.

The man grinned and said, "Can I give you boys a lift?"

Pastor Walker smiled.

"That would be wonderful."

Melvin spat again, the tobacco juice hitting the pavement with a muted splat. And then from years of practice, Melvin maneuvered the tow truck in front of the pickup, and prepared to hitch us up.

I went to get out of the cab, but Walker grabbed my arm.

"There's something else I need to tell you," he said, his eyes wide with renewed alarm.

"There's more?"

He nodded and let go of my arm.

"Natasha's the one who told me where to get the loan."

"But what does she have to do with it?" I asked. I wanted an explanation.

Then the pieces fell into place in my head. The money for the church. The late payments. The visit from the Boston money guys. The trafficking operation. I stiffened, an image of Anna bound and gagged screaming its way into my head.

"It was my ex-wife's friend who gave me the money." He looked up at me, real fear blotching his complexion, and tears gathering in the corners of his eyes. He said, "Natasha's family bankrolls the entire operation, and now they have Anna."

CHAPTER TWELVE

I stared at Walker for a long moment. What sort of twisted web had I fallen into? I had questions, but now wasn't the time. Melvin the tow truck driver was watching us as he hitched up the pickup.

"We'll talk when we get back to your place," I said, my heart pounding at the thought of Anna falling into her mother's hands. I promised myself in that millisecond that I would do anything in my power to return her to safety. The beast in me grinned.

THE RIDE back took longer than expected. Maybe it was my impatience or maybe it was the fact that Melvin, whose body odor did an impressive job of filling the cramped cab, was in no particular hurry. He chatted away with Pastor Walker, informing the church leader about who got a DUI over the weekend, and that Mrs. Brambleton had fallen and broken her hip. He ignored me, and I him. I chose to look out the window and let Walker keep the man distracted.

The tow truck hadn't even stopped when I burst from the cab and made for the guest house.

"Nice meeting you, too!" Melvin called after me.

I answered by slamming the door behind me.

Pastor Walker came in a couple minutes later. I was in the middle of taking stock of my belongings. There wasn't much. It was pathetic, really. The entirety of my personal belongings that I kept in my rucksack lay on the bed. Well-worn clothes, a half-empty bottle of Jack Daniels, my lock pick set, and a tattered magazine I'd picked up some time in the past week. I didn't have a phone. My wallet held my old military ID card, an ATM card, a credit card, and a driver's license. I didn't even have a knife, let alone a gun.

"Sit," I said, pointing to the chair in the corner without looking up. My mind was still processing what our next move —scratch that—what *my* next move should be. If anything, Pastor Walker had proven himself to be a worthless teammate and a failure as a dad. In my head, what needed to be done could easily be accomplished without him.

He did as commanded, and I stuffed my belongings back into the bag.

"Do you know where your ex lives?" I asked, my brain shifting into operational mode. I needed intel.

"Somewhere in Boston," Walker answered lamely.

I shook my head in disgust, but held back the snide comment I could've shot his way.

"Tell me again how you know where to pick up the girls."

"I get a call and someone tells me where to go. Sometimes I take a cab and sometimes I get a ride. When I get there I get the keys to whatever vehicle they've got and I come straight back here."

"When do they tell you how many girls there will be?"

"During the initial call."

I turned from my things and pointed a finger at him.

"Here's how this works, Pastor. When I ask you a question, tell me everything that comes to mind. I don't care how mundane you think the detail is, you tell me. We don't have time for me to ask you a thousand questions. Now, tell me everything they told you in that initial phone call."

Walker nodded and said, "They tell me where to go, what time to be there and how many girls to prep the shelter for."

"Okay. And how about the back end? They call to tell you where to take them, right?"

"They do," he answered. He continued, thankfully remembering my previous instructions. "I get a call, usually a day or two later, the longest was a week, and they tell me where to go."

"No other demands, like extra things to bring with you or what state the girls should be in?"

"No. As long as I give them the medication with their food, that seems to do the trick."

I'd almost forgotten about the drugs.

"Have they ever told you what's in the medication?" I asked.

"I questioned them once, but they told me it was none of my business. From what I've observed, it seems to be a rather mild narcotic."

"You have much experience with drugs?"

Walker nodded. "From my time in Boston and the occasional drug addict that stumbles into my church."

His answer reminded me that this man wasn't naive to the evils of the world, just clueless about his role in it. I'd realized that on the way home, and wondered how many people lived their lives that way, going along with things because they felt like they had no control over anything. That's what my gut told me anyway: that Pastor Walker, while not an evil man, had succumbed to evil nonetheless. It wasn't my place to change him, but a small piece of me hoped he would come to see that he did have a choice, that everyone has a choice unless they were chained to a wall in a windowless prison cell. But even those people had choices, the main one being whether to keep on living or just give up.

That line of thinking made me shiver, the reality hitting too close to home. I hadn't gone that route yet, but there'd been ample opportunity. Luckily for me, the two-sided coin kept landing in my favor. One day it wouldn't, and I was okay with that.

For now there was work to do, and I tried to think of something I could ask the pastor that might give us some clue as to where Anna had been taken.

"What about the pickup and drop-off locations? Are they ever the same?"

"No."

"What kinds of places are they?"

"Out of the way. Places like here. There's plenty of vacant land in the surrounding states." But then I saw it, a flicker of something in his eyes, like he'd just remembered something.

"What is it? What did you just think of?" I asked.

His face twisted in thought, and then he said, "There was this one time where the drop-off changed. I was on my way there and I got a text with a new address."

"Where was it?"

"It was an address in Boston."

My pulse quickened.

"Had there ever been a delivery in Boston?"

"No."

"So why did they change this one?"

"They didn't say, but when I got there things were more rushed than usual, like something had spooked them. I didn't recognize any of the guys, like they were using another crew."

"And where was it? Where was the drop-off?" I asked, finally smelling the beginning of a lead.

"That was the weird thing. It was a car wash. Usually they take the vehicle and give me a ride to somewhere I can catch a cab. This time I got out at the car wash entrance and they told me to go through the lobby and wait. I did, and when they gave me the van again, the back was empty."

"What did you do with the van?"

"They told me to take it someplace downtown and leave the keys in the ignition. I left it two blocks from the first place I'd lived in the city."

"What was it called?"

"The place I left the van?"

"No," I said, "What was the car wash called?"

He pursed his lips thinking, and then said, "It was something with shine or...wait, Sunshine Car Wash. Yeah, that's what it was. Sunshine Car Wash."

"Do you remember how to get there?"

"No, but I can look it up on my computer." He rose to do just that, but I held up a hand.

"We'll do that next."

His face scrunched in confusion.

I answered his question before he could ask.

"First, you need to make a call."

I watched him gulp slowly, but he nodded and asked, "Who do you want me to call?"

I crossed my arms and said, "It's time to call your ex-wife."

CHAPTER THIRTEEN

He didn't flinch. Two points for the good pastor. He slid his dented cell phone out of his pocket, holding it with two fingers like it was going to bite him. I expected him to fetch the phone number from the house, but he didn't. Pastor Walker dialed it from memory.

I put my head next to his as the other line rang once, twice, and then a third time. A female voice that oozed a certain haughty air—or was it disdain?—came on the line after the fourth ring.

"Hello, Eddie," she said. They were two words, two words that conveyed her mood like a punch in the face. Her tone was proper, like a foreigner trying to mask a childhood accent. Walker did flinch this time. I did have to squeeze his arm so he would remember to talk.

"Hello, Natasha," he somehow got out.

"I must say, Eddie, you've done a horrible job with your business, but you've somehow managed to raise a lovely young lady. Then again, who knows how much of that came inherently from her mother."

Both of our bodies tensed, and I sensed that Walker might panic.

"Is she there? Is Anna okay?" he asked, his voice thick with desperation.

"Oh, she's fine. She was quite exhausted from her little ordeal. I told her to take a cat nap and then I'd take her shopping."

"I need her back, Natasha. She belongs with me."

A low chuckle came over the line and she said, "I'll have to think about that, Eddie. Papa's been pestering me about getting Anna back. This might be the perfect time. I could show her the business. From what I've seen of her, she seems very bright, maybe almost as smart as me."

"Natasha, please. She's all I have. If you take her from me..."

"No!" The word cracked in our ears like a high power rifle. "You were given one simple task, one mindless duty that would ensure your livelihood and the funding for your puny church. But what did you do? You somehow allowed my daughter to find out." She chuckled again, her tone mellowing. "You really haven't changed, have you, Eddie? Still the simple boy from backwoods North Dakota."

"Montana," Walker corrected.

"Whatever. I don't know what I ever saw in you." She sighed and said, "Well, I must go. There's so much to do. Please have your phone handy, Eddie. I'm sure you'll be receiving another delivery very soon."

"Let me talk to Anna," Walker said, gripping the phone so hard it knocked into my head. "Natasha? Natasha!"

"She hung up," I said.

He stared at me like a beaten man, and for the second time that day I got a glimpse into his world. I could see her comment about ever falling for him hit hard. He had loved her deeply. I'd never known that kind of love for a woman.

There'd never been time. Between training and deployments, I'd never found the right match.

I empathized with his situation. How would I have turned out if I'd been born in Walker's body? How is a kid raised in Montana?

I never had the loving upbringing like a lot of friends, but at least I'd found the Corps. It shaped me into the man I was, for good or bad. It gave me three hot meals a day, training, and a family. More than anything, it taught me how to tough it out, that any obstacle could be overcome. Maybe the pastor had never had that. It made the anger I'd felt for him lessen half a step.

"Hey, I need to borrow a razor and a comb."

My request shook him from his misery.

"What? Why?" he asked.

I grinned, hoping my attitude would soon pass confidence onto the only ally I had at the moment.

"I'm going to get a job."

———

IN ADDITION TO THE RAZOR, shaving cream and comb, Pastor Walker also scrounged up a two year old Buick from a neighbor. He even ran to her house to get it while I got ready.

When I stepped out of the guest house, the car was idling and thankfully looked a thousand times more reliable than the pickup truck. Walker was in the driver's seat and motioned for me to get in. Instead, I walked over to the driver's side and told him to get out.

"I can drive," he said.

"I'm going by myself."

"But..."

"Don't worry, Pastor, I'm a good driver," I said, sliding

into the squeaky clean leather seat. "Stay here and man the phones. I'll call you when I get a new cell."

"And you'll tell me what's happening?"

I nodded and shifted the car into drive.

"Daniel?" he said.

"Yeah?"

Hesitation there, like he wanted to ask me something critical, something that would turn the tide in our favor. But he didn't. He just said, "You clean up good."

I smiled, gave him a reaffirming nod, and took off down the driveway.

THE ADDRESS we found for Sunshine Car Wash wasn't actually in the city of Boston at all. It was in a suburb called Amesbury, a well-to-do area that lay north of the city and the Merrimack River. Google said it was about an hour drive from Old Orchard Beach. From the pictures on Google, it seemed like the last place a criminal organization would set up shop. Then again, looks could be deceiving. I was proof of that fact, and I was about to make it even better.

There was a Wal-Mart on the way, just off of Interstate 95. No way a respectful community like Amesbury would house a Wal-Mart. God forbid.

This Wal-Mart was a mirror image to the many I'd been in over the years. The aisles were clean, well kept, and shoppers bustled back and forth. No one gave me a second glance as I gathered what I needed. This was a scouting mission, so even though I would've loved to start in the outdoors department, I stuck to the men's clothing section.

I tried everything on, exchanged a large for a medium t-shirt, and then paid with cash. After changing in the restroom, I ditched my old clothes in the bottom of the waste basket. My boots were in the plastic shopping bag. I'd need those later.

I gave myself one last look in the mirror, running a hand through my blonde hair then over my clean shaven face. Passable.

MY FIRST DRIVE by took me through the center of downtown Amesbury. It felt like going back in time. Lots of two story brick buildings and matching sidewalks. I wondered how many time-period movies had been filmed there. I could easily imagine Ben Franklin clicking down the way or John Adams strolling around the traditional traffic circle. Time had given way to money. You could smell it. Old money. Maybe back to the American Revolution type money.

I'd never had much money, but it didn't bother me. This was just another town on my endless journey. The only difference was that this town had a destination, a target. I found my objective a block off the main square. Another block and a half down from there, Sunshine Car Wash sat gleaming and new. They'd knocked down a house to finish construction. I could see that much from the look of the residential strip surrounding it.

The car wash slipped by and I cruised on. I'd seen a public parking lot a few blocks back and decided to stash the car there. The car wasn't part of my disguise.

I WALKED into Sunshine Car Wash fifteen minutes later, in stylish baggy pants, a fluorescent t-shirt and skater kicks. The place was empty except for a chubby girl behind the counter who was chatting away on the store's phone line with one eye on the soap opera on the corner television. She didn't even hear me come in she was talking so loudly.

I was glad it was a girl behind the counter. It wasn't that women were more gullible; in fact, a lot of times they were more suspicious than their male counterparts. But this one was a perfect play. She'd been pretty once, and she spoke with the air of someone who'd been important, even if that was only head cheerleader.

Her clothes were cute but two sizes too small and matched her overdone makeup that screamed, "Look at me!" A discarded brown bakery wrapper sat on the desk in front of her, a super-sized coffee next to it.

Late twenties, I thought. Well past her prime. Perfect.

I had to cough in my hand twice to get her attention. The second cough earned me an annoyed look as she whipped her head around. The look changed to interest, and then she said into the phone, "Let me call you back, Claire."

She sat the phone back in its cradle gently. My face shifted into an easy smile.

"Can I help you?" she asked.

I ran a hand through my hair like I was embarrassed and trying to keep cool.

"Yeah. I was wondering if you guys are hiring."

She tapped a long fingernail against her lips and looked me up and down.

"Are you new in town?"

"Uh huh."

She actually licked her lips and said, "What kind of experience do you have?"

I shrugged like I didn't want to answer, and then said, "I was in the Marines."

Oh, she fluttered at that. She even blushed.

"I *looove* Marines. You're all so handsome. Did you go to war?"

Why did civilians always think that was an appropriate

question? I ignored the bitterness in my gut and shrugged again like I didn't want to talk about it.

She smiled wider. I wondered if she thought she'd just caught her knight in shining armor, a real hero. *Sorry, lady, that's not me.*

"Well, thank you so much for your service," she said sweetly, like she really cared. It was another throwaway comment that had quickly pervaded American culture. I hated hearing it.

"Thanks," I said. "So, about a job?"

She waved her hands in the air and reached down and opened a drawer, shuffling papers until she produced a single sheet.

"I'm Florence, by the way," she said, extending her puffy hand.

I shook it, and said, "Like Florence Nightingale." She scrunched her face in confusion, so I added, "She was a nurse, took care of soldiers and stuff. Really famous."

Her eyes brightened at once. "Oh, I'll have to Google that!"

She would too, if for no other reason than to further her own self-importance, something to brag about. I smiled.

"What did you say your name was, honey?" she asked.

"Sorry. My name's Brad." We shook hands again. This time I held onto hers a little bit longer, even giving her a little squeeze at the end. I saw her shiver.

You might think it was a cruel trick, something I shouldn't do, but when the mission calls for a guy to use his natural gifts, namely a good looking face, I am not above doing it. Besides, she reminded me of a girl in middle school who'd hounded me for weeks, always coming up with some clever taunt to giggle about with her friends. I had run into that girl years later. Let's just say she'd aged about as well as Florence. It made it easy to use every ounce of charm I had.

Her gaze lingered on my face, and then shifted to my arms, then back to my face. She smiled, this time almost shyly.

"Well, Brad, right now is kind of our slow time. Not much going on. The guys we do have working spend more time playing cards in the back than drying cars." She tapped her lips again, all business now. "But I'm the assistant manager, and one of the guys said he might be quitting soon. How long will you be in town?"

"I'm not sure. Like I said, I just got here. Been traveling a lot, but I ran out of money. Need to restock my cash, you know?"

She nodded thoughtfully.

"Tell you what, why don't I give you a quick tour and tell you about our payroll plan as we walk?"

I nodded eagerly. She'd just said the magic words.

THE PLACE WASN'T BIG, but she somehow stretched the tour into thirty minutes. During that time she used every opportunity to touch my arm, or guide me through a door by pushing my lower back. Her touch never lingered, but it was always there. Florence's exhaustive description of the place included every employee's name, the exact process for washing towels, and the precise number of gallons used for each of the five packages available for car washes.

Sprinkled throughout the tour were little comments about her wicked ex-boyfriend, how good she was at karaoke and that she might try out for one of those singing shows. Finally, she talked about how she'd not only been a cheerleader, but even Homecoming Queen. Like I said, past her prime.

She showed me every closet, nook and wash bay. The

place couldn't have been more than two thousand square feet, but she milked every inch.

There was only one room we didn't go into and I asked her about it.

"Oh, that's the owner's private office. He doesn't like anyone going in there."

I pretended like I didn't care, but the beast shivered inside. I was close.

WHEN THE TOUR WAS OVER, Florence gave me the application reluctantly (I'd told her that I still had to get a new driver's license before I could properly apply). The door dinged when the first customer since I'd been there walked in. Florence looked annoyed, but did her best to plaster a fake smile on her face.

"I'll be right with you," she said to the man, who nodded and sidled up to the counter.

"So you'll be back tomorrow?" she asked me.

"As long as the DMV doesn't give me a hard time," I joked. "I'll even see if I can get it done today." There was hope in her eyes, like I'd just made her day, again. "Do you mind if I use the bathroom before I go?"

Her eyebrow arched lasciviously, teasing, and then she smiled. "Sure. You remember where it is?"

How could I not? It was one of only three actual rooms in the place.

"Yeah, thanks."

The bathroom smelled like peaches and I heard the air freshener puff after I locked the door. I figured I had five minutes. Hopefully it wouldn't take near that long. This was only a recon, after all.

I'd been surprised to see that the interior had all drop ceilings. Someone once told me it had to do with energy conservation, but to me it was just one more place to get away, hide, or go from room to room. It was exactly what I'd been hoping for.

I popped the ceiling panel that was closest to the outer wall and pulled myself up. It still smelled new in the three foot space, like a construction site. The tiles would never hold my weight, so I crawled over the tops of where the walls supported part of the ceiling. A minute later I was looking down at the tiles covering the locked office, the owner's space. That's when I got my first surprise. These squares weren't set in the ceiling like the others. The tiles over the owner's office were secured by steel and the screws were set from below. No way was I getting through unless I busted one out. Not a good idea.

Time ticked by as I considered my options. Then it hit me. My lock pick kit.

Thirty seconds later I'd managed to jimmy a tiny hole in the chalky mineral fiber tile.

Three minutes, rang the timer in my head.

Luck was with me again. There was no one in the office, but the lights were on. A desk with a computer in the corner. A lounge chair. My one eye shifted to the opposite side of the room. I froze. It might've seemed innocent to someone else. A joke really. But my vision saw it as something else. As I looked at the fancy dart board, white numbers half-erased from the scoring tables on either side, my gaze rested on one thing, mounted to the center of the board. No, not mounted; pinned with three darts adorned with Russian flag fletches. It was the smiling face of a man I knew, his black pastor's garb impossible to miss.

Pastor Ed Walker was in deeper shit than I'd thought.

I HEARD the knocking on the bathroom door before I got

back to the open tile. Hurrying that way, I cursed at myself for not buying a phone at Wal-Mart. If I had I could've called Walker.

Right now I had another problem. The knocking grew more insistent than before. I imagined one of the workers fetching the key and bursting in, stranding me in three feet of dead space, or worse, dropping in at the exact time he walked in.

I eased down and shifted the tile into place, calling, "Almost done," as I stepped off the toilet. Unzipping my fly and skewing my shirt like I'd just gotten up, I flushed the toilet and moved to the door. When I opened it, Florence's face greeted me. "Hey, sorry," I said.

She wasn't embarrassed. In fact, there was a glimmer in her eyes. She looked down at my unzipped fly. My hand reached down and zipped it.

"I was just coming to see if you needed any help," she purred, her swollen lips pouty and glossed. Her hand reached out and she unzipped my fly. "So, do you need any help?" She really played it up, even batting her eyes at me.

I grinned and grabbed her brazen hand, bringing it to my lips.

"Rain check?" I asked, kissing the back of her hand. Her mouth dropped open and she nodded mutely. "I'll be back in the morning. Maybe you can show me around town." Another nod. No words. I kissed her hand again and then moved past the sex-starved assistant manager.

There were things to do, and none of them involved Florence Nightingale.

CHAPTER FOURTEEN

Open. Close.
            Open. Close.

Her eyes clicked through the rhythm, snapshots of the same spot of the thick crown molding overhead. She was supposed to be sleeping. There were a lot of things she was "supposed" to do.

She was supposed to do what she was told.

She was supposed to act like a normal teenager.

She was supposed to...

Anna huffed in frustration, her mind drifting back to the image of her mother: sleek, elegant, powerful. She'd watched as drivers and helpers deferred to Miss Varushkin. She'd even heard one man call her *Duchess*. The excitement in her belly tingled just thinking about that word. Could her mother really be royalty? She looked like it. Natasha Varushkin was exactly how Anna had imagined the regal aristocracy of pre-World War I Russia, before Lenin, Stalin and the rest of the Communists.

She'd read plenty on her family's homeland. There seemed to be so much beauty combined with a healthy slathering of corruption and secrecy. But that had never frightened Anna. The opposite was true. Her study of the Cold War only heightened the pull.

Of course, she wanted to go to Paris, Rome and the rest of the world's landmark centers of culture, but she'd always secretly wanted to go to Moscow, and maybe even take a dog sled through Siberia, wrapped in expensive furs, the frigid wind her constant companion.

She'd never told her father about those dreams. While he supported her "normal" dreams, any discussion of her mother or her mother's familial past met with a funny comment that diverted the conversation away from his painful memories.

But now she was close to her mother. She was in her mother's guest room in her expensive condo overlooking Boston Harbor. It wasn't Moscow, or even St. Petersburg, but it felt a universe away from Old Orchard Beach, Maine.

That made her think about her dad and how worried he must be. But her mom said she'd take care of it, that they would spend time together, just the girls. Her mother said the decision was hers as to where she went afterwards.

When Anna had asked about the girls she'd rescued, her mother informed Anna that the girls were already safely in the hands of the authorities.

That put her mind at rest about the poor girls, but it still didn't assuage her fears about her father. Would the police arrest him? She'd have to ask her mother about that. Maybe there was something that could be done to explain why he'd done it. If someone made him do it, there was no way he could take all the blame.

In her head, Anna went down that path, imagining how the investigation might go, her possible role in it, and the likely outcomes. She'd seen enough detective shows to know that what the cops really wanted was the main bad guys, and not the poor pastor who was being blackmailed into doing what he'd done. That made Anna smile. It would be a hard road, but with the help of God and her mother, Anna had faith that everything would figure itself out in the end.

So as she finally dozed off, her thought bounced from her mother, to her father, and then another face appeared in the darkness. Daniel. *Where is Daniel?*

————

"WHEN WILL IT BE DONE?" Natasha Varushkin asked.

"This evening," said the man sitting across from her. He was Russian, but like his boss, there wasn't even a hint of an accent. In fact, he didn't even look Russian. His fair skin and sandy hair made him right at home with the Irish population in Boston.

"Good." Natasha sipped the tea in her glass and glanced at the well-stocked bar. For a moment she considered getting a real drink. That wouldn't do. She fought hard for her sobriety. Multiple stints in rehab had taught her to regain control of her life, that the bottle was never the answer. She smiled when she thought about all that she'd accomplished since finding sobriety. It was the reason she'd been elevated to her current position within The Pension, and she knew it would be one of the many reasons her father would soon name her as his successor. "Tell me when it is done," she said, nodding to her lieutenant as he rose from his chair and left the room.

The issue with her ex-husband was a small thing in comparison to what would soon transpire. Although, the thought of having her daughter close by might increase her value in the eyes of her father. He'd always chided her for giving up custody, and had even offered to pay for the custody hearings over the years. But she hadn't been ready. Natasha was gifted in so many ways, and yet, certain aspects of her life had always held her back.

That was no longer the case. She was in control.

Natasha had been the one to purge The Pension of low-life thugs and petty criminals. Instead of flashy cars and shiny suits, Pension associates now worked hard to blend in with the latest upper middle class fashions. They lived on quiet streets in lazy suburbs. They drove American cars and were involved in community sports and small business.

Let their foolish cousins prance around in Armani suits, live in New York penthouses and jet set in hundred-million dollar planes. It made them easy targets, and the fact that they invested in American companies and touted themselves as the "new Russians" did little to hide what they really were: criminals masked in Prada sunglasses. Fools.

The final pieces were finally being played. The Pension was well-entrenched, their future almost secured. All that needed to happen was for their leader to arrive and take his rightful place at the head of The Pension.

Yes, Natasha thought, *it will be good to have father home*.

CHAPTER FIFTEEN

The cruise ship's sun deck was deserted except for the lone figure who sat wrapped in a blanket, gazing out over the endless ocean. Wind whipped his weathered face, and the occasional gust of sea spray sometimes came high enough to mist his vision, but he did not care. If anything, the ocean was greeting him, a long lost friend, a comrade who'd braved Poseidon's tempests and lingered in tropical calms.

Georgy Varushkin was a man of the sea. His father was a fisherman, and Georgy's earliest memories all included the smell of the catch or the pitch of a deck. But the quiet life in the protected cove off the Caspian Sea was never enough for young Georgy. With his father's blessing (and most likely a healthy prodding from his mother), Georgy enlisted in the Soviet Navy, thinking it would lead to adventure and a better life than that of his father.

At that time, in the mid-1960s, the Soviet Navy sailed proud, its warships and submarines playing the ultimate game of survival against the Americans. Georgy knew, barely a year into his enlistment, that he'd been naive. While he respected the institution and believed in its mission, his intellect alienated him from his peers. They were simple men, used to the hard toil of life underway. Georgy had always worked hard, but when he wasn't helping his father, he was either curled up with a book or rushing to school.

He climbed the enlisted ranks as if on fire, passing sailors who'd spent many years at the same job, on the same ship. Looking back, he realized that not only had his work ethic and education helped him, it had been the benevolent gaze of certain officers who recognized his talent. Not yet two years into his initial enlistment, Georgy Varushkin found himself in front of a board of officers where he was questioned at length about not only his skills as an enlisted man, but also about his family and about his allegiance to the Soviet Union.

Weeks went by and he heard nothing. Just as he passed it off as a fluke, thinking maybe others had been through the same interview, he was summoned to the captain's quarters. He reported in on shaky legs. The captain of the ship was there, along with one of the officers who'd been on the board. The captain informed him to pack his belongings. He would soon be receiving an officer's commission as a Sub-lieutenant, along with a world class education.

Rather than send him to the academy, or perhaps one of its smaller sub schools, he was passed from command to command, always reporting to a single senior officer. He worked hard, and soon had a solid view of everything the Soviet Navy beheld. There was only one caveat. Each time he reported to a new six-month stint, he was told by his mentor not to discuss his "situation" with any other junior officers, and especially not the enlisted men. The request seemed strange for the first time or two, but then he was swept away by this warrant officer or that engineering chief to see the bowels of the latest nuclear behemoth.

By the end of his fourth year of on-the-job education, Lieutenant Varushkin had spent time with the Navy's surface forces, submarine fleets, aviation component, and even a brutal six-month stint with the Naval Infantry.

He remembered it now with fondness; his early years in the Navy had taught him so much about life. There had been a reason for his unusual education, but he wouldn't come to find that reason for almost a decade. Sometimes he wished he could have remained a simple sailor, maybe even retiring to a quiet life of fishing like his father. But such dreams were wasted. Great men were accorded great destinies.

He'd paid for his destiny, including his most recent five year stay in a maximum security political prison just outside Moscow. It was so secret that there had once even been a McDonald's three stories above it. His time there had been easy. It was the periodic journeys to a laundry list of some of Russia's worst Gulags that had done the real toll. He still shivered when he thought about those sleepless nights, never knowing when the systematic torture would begin again, or when the cell block's most sadistic prisoner would be allowed into his cell for a little play time.

They'd almost killed him once, and after that, the beatings were only administered by the president's cronies disguised as prison guards. He'd always known the difference, could see it in their eyes, the cunning and the intelligence.

Georgy rubbed his arms and pulled the fleece blanket up to his chin. What he would have given for such a luxury as a soft blanket. His first night on a bed in the cruise ship's posh suite had lasted ten minutes. He knew because he'd counted them as they passed on the gold clock next to the bed. After that, he'd slept on the floor, huddling with a pillow and a sheet, the only things he'd managed to grab as his emaciated frame slipped to the ground.

"Your dinner is ready, Captain," came the familiar voice from behind his bench. Varushkin turned to find his man waiting, hands holding onto a wheelchair.

"Thank you, Vasily."

His steward nodded and wheeled the handicap device around.

The thing with his legs was new. One morning, maybe a month before, he'd awoken to find that he could no longer move his legs. The guards hadn't offered to take him to a doctor, and he had never asked. Instead, his ever-faithful friend Vasily, a former sailor who'd been one of his stewards on his final ship, fetched a wheelchair and pushed him wherever they were ordered to go.

Vasily did the same now, taking care to lift his former commander's 136-pound body in a way that would not knock him into the railing or the chair. Varushkin wondered what kind of fate had delivered this man to him. What power in heaven had allowed the two men to meet in prison and form a bond that they'd both so desperately needed? For a time he'd thought it all a ruse, that maybe his captors had placed Vasily there to spy on him. But Varushkin still had friends, and those friends confirmed that Vasily's appearance was a simple coincidence.

Luckily, by the efforts of those same friends, Varushkin's release had been brokered, along with the guarantee that Vasily be let go as well. Upon hearing of his freedom, Vasily had sworn his life to the former Soviet Navy Captain 1st Rank. The solemn ceremony had reminded the historically inclined Varushkin of the knights of old, swearing allegiance to their lord and protector. There had been tears in his eyes when he'd accepted Vasily's promise, and the two men embraced like old comrades, too emotional to give formal handshakes.

And so here they were, on a luxury cruise ship bound for America. He'd been promised safe passage, and so far he'd gotten it. Five years in Russian prisons had given him a healthy sense of doom, and for the first four days of their journey he'd expected that the ship would turn around, someone would simply push him off, or that maybe a Russian fighter would swoop down and destroy the entire vessel.

None of that had happened and as they cruised closer to the American coast, Georgy Varushkin felt freedom inch closer. Mother Russia had changed. If it hadn't been for that ill-conceived journey home, he never would have seen it in its entirety. But now he saw it all, how his training and the career-long mentorship of his benefactors had shaped his mind into what it had become.

And now, billions of dollars were being filtered through hundreds of funnels that flowed into the holdings of The Pension. America was the perfect birthplace: A land where money was respected, where politicians could be bent but not outright corrupted, and where the citizenry was by and large honest and good. They'd explored other options, like Switzerland and even China, but Varushkin always believed that America held the most promise. He'd finally won the rest over. America it would be.

And so, as Vasily wheeled him down to supper, Georgy Varushkin dreamed of a new chance with his family beside him and the world at their fingertips. Yes, it was a good dream, maybe even the best. Georgy Varushkin smiled inwardly, still unaccustomed to showing outward emotion, an unfortunate byproduct of his imprisonment. He meant to change that soon with the help of his daughter, the dazzling Natasha, and the young girl whose picture he'd first seen that morning: his only grandchild, Anna.

CHAPTER SIXTEEN

The call from Daniel was short and to the point.

"Get out, now."

Pastor Ed Walker stuffed the few things he thought he'd need into an old day pack, a throwback to his hiking days. Those days had long passed, and yet the feel of the straps on his shoulders brought back a deluge of memories, like it was his vessel back into the unknown. As he went to grab the handle to the back door, he had a thought. Rushing back to his office, he unlocked the safe and grabbed his pistol and a few loose rounds. He wasn't the best shot, but maybe Daniel could use it. The gun, wrapped in one of his favorite t-shirts, went into the pack with the rest of his gear.

His task accomplished, Walker took one last look around the only place he'd really considered home in a very long time. There'd been good times, like Anna's giggles as she cooked her latest concoction and her father retold some obscure story from his past. She thought he was a little hokey —okay, a lot hokey—but what teenager didn't think that of their ancient dad?

Those memories clouded suddenly, darker images

replacing the lighter pinks and greens. They were the memories of lost souls, the poor girls he'd carted on and off his property. He could no longer blame it on bad luck or possibly God's will. No, it was time for him to take responsibility.

He spoke of responsibility often in church, expounding the benefits of taking charge of one's life and staring evil in the eye. *Hypocrite*, he thought. For years, he'd sought perfection from his parishioners, but the one who really needed saving was the man standing behind the pulpit. It shamed him. It humbled him. His heart lay splayed, ready to accept judgment. Funny that Daniel, a vagabond with a wandering soul, would be the one to call him out.

Pastor Walker envied Daniel's conviction even while he saw the demons dancing inside the young man's chest. Maybe together they could find forgiveness, clarity, peace. The prayer was still on his lips when he heard the crunching gravel from the front yard.

He didn't think, just ran, taking a route toward the backwoods that would keep him from view. As he passed under the protective shade of the tree line, Pastor Walker looked back to see the van with a flashy security company logo pasted along its side pull up to the house. He noted the name of the company and plunged deeper into the woods. He had a schedule to keep.

———

ADAM EPLAR GRABBED the tool kit from the back of the van and walked to the house. He tried the doorbell first. No answer. He knocked next. Still no answer. He made one pass around the house calling out, "Mr. Walker? Anyone home?" Nothing.

No cars in the driveway, no signs of life inside or out.

The back door was unlocked. He stepped in, sniffing the

air out of habit. Old house. Turn of the century. Lots of wood. No sound except for the creaking of the hardwood floor under his feet.

"Mr. Walker?" Adam called out again. "I'm here from the security company."

No answer.

He cleared the house in five minutes. No one home.

He slid the cell phone from his pocket and put it to his ear, the call already going through.

"The place is empty," he said when the answering click came on the line. "Do you want me to wait?"

There was a pause and then a voice said, "No. Burn it down, and then do the same with the shelter in the woods."

Adam heard another click and replaced the phone in his pocket. He was a little disappointed. Things had been pretty boring for a while now. The bosses said it was a sign of things to come. Adam Eplar wasn't sure what that meant, but he did worry about his skills going to shit. He'd have to renew his membership at that local gun club. No sense in letting all that hard work go to waste.

From his coat pocket he pulled the pistol and aimed it at the smiling picture of Pastor Walker sitting on the living room table. Adam had a copy of the same picture in his office. He imagined squeezing the trigger and watching the glass frame shatter. He smiled and put the gun away. Hopefully, there would be time for that later. Word in the organization was that the guy was the Duchess's ex-husband. *Lucky bastard*, Adam thought, and then went back to the van to get what he needed.

———

NOT MUCH LONGER, I thought, rubbing my hands together to fight off the early evening chill. I'd stood guard for four hours, watching the occasional customer pull into the Sunshine Car Wash bay, and leave five minutes later with a newly clean car. There was never a line, and pretty soon Florence or someone higher up the chain made the decision to start letting the workers go. I saw one and then another familiar face get into a car, and take off away from Amesbury.

Florence was the last one to leave, waddling her way to a maroon Toyota Corolla with princess stickers all over the back window. Her cell phone never left her ear as she got in and drove away. I wondered if she was bragging to one of her friends, telling them that she was going to get it on with a blond stranger who'd just happened to walk into her store.

The phone I'd picked up at a local drug store buzzed. It was the only person in the world who knew the number, Pastor Walker.

"Yeah?" I answered, anxious to hear that he'd gotten away safely.

"I made it out." Then there was a pause, and a grunt, like he was stepping over something and then he said, "Someone showed up in a van just as I was leaving."

I nodded to myself.

"Who was it?"

"A security company called Samson Security. I didn't catch the plates."

"Did you stick around to see who was in it?"

A small hesitation and he answered, "No, you told me to run, so I did."

"Good. How long do you think it'll take you to get to Boston?"

I'd come up with the plan to have Walker get a hotel room downtown, something off the main drag that didn't cost too much. We'd meet there once I finished at the car wash.

"Probably two hours," he said, grunting again. I imagined

him traipsing through the woods in the darkness, avoiding branches and logs like a city slicker.

"Okay. I may be here a while. I'll call when I'm on my way. Oh, and Pastor?"

"Yes?"

"Watch your step out there. I need you in one piece, okay?"

"I'll do my best."

I ended the call and set the phone back on my lap. As my eyes shifted back to the car wash, I began reciting my stay-awake-list in my head, which included the memorable guys from my boot camp platoon. *Recruit Finn, the one with the mole on his ass. Recruit Rice, the one who stuttered. Recruit Islander, the one who was always praying.*

I'D MADE it through the list six times when the van showed up. It screamed *Samson Security* in red and black lettering on the side. The vehicle wrap looked untarnished and new under the car wash lights. Instead of pulling into one of the spots in front of the entrance, the van pulled up into the first bay, and I saw a guy get out and unlock the garage style door, slide it up, then get back into the van and pull it in. The sliding door went back down a few seconds later, the driver and van safely inside.

I got up from my post behind the large oak tree, and stretched the soreness out of my legs. Time to see what Mr. Security Van knew.

———

ADAM LOCKED the garage bay door behind him, and flicked on the bay lights. He'd never imagined owning a car wash, but that's where he'd ended up. Not that he actually owned it, but according to the Registrar of Deeds, Adam S. Eplar did indeed own the parcel of land and the improvements of said property.

He didn't have to do much with the business. It pretty much ran itself and he only had to occasionally jump someone's ass for screwing up a piece of the operation. As long as the cars were washed and the insides were detailed, customers were happy and that meant Adam was happy.

Adam hadn't understood the wisdom of running his other business out of a car wash until they'd actually made use of it. There were always shipments of some sort, and the simple building was an easy cover for such transactions. Another benefit that had quickly become apparent was the ability to house and change a variety of vehicles. That's what he had to do now. The large sticker with Samson Security had to come off tonight, the exterior prepped, and then the next morning, a separate crew would come in and apply a new full body wrap, completely transforming the white van into a delivery vehicle for a popular video game store.

If he had more manpower at the moment, Adam wouldn't have had to get his hands dirty, but every last extra man they had was being used in preparation for some important arrival. He didn't know what it was all about, other than the stern orders from his superiors and the reassignment of his available men.

Adam put the thought aside and flipped on the radio in the corner. He bobbed his head as Mick Jagger kicked on with his languid love sling, "Beast of Burden."

I'll never be your beast of burden.
I've walked for miles, my feet are hurting.

HE SANG along as the heat gun warmed in his hand and he worked the stream over the top corner of the Samson Security sticker.

Am I hard enough?
Am I rough enough?
Am I rich enough?

ADAM LOVED THOSE LINES. Even though it was supposed to be a love song, it reminded him of the miles and miles he'd marched in the Russian cold, his feet close to frostbite and belly rumbling from hunger. He'd come a long way since then, even donning a new name and painstakingly wiping his old accent from memory.

His grin disappeared when he felt cold hard metal jabbing into the back of his neck. He froze. He'd been robbed once before, but that had been in Boston by some cracked out Irishman looking for an easy score. The man had gotten away, but he'd been found a week later in a puddle of his own blood in an abandoned row house.

"The money's in the register," Adam said calmly, raising his hands over his head.

"I don't want your money," said the equally calm voice.

"Then what do you want?"

"Tell me about Natasha Varushkin."

Adam tensed. *Shit*, he thought. *How did this guy get into my shop?*

Adam's shoulder sagged an inch and he pretended to turn around slowly. Halfway into it, however, he picked up speed and his leg bent in order to avoid the bullet aimed at his head. It was a long shot, but Adam had been in similar scraps before. Usually it was all about who made the first move, and Adam Eplar wasn't about to get shot in the back.

The first thing he noticed was the guy's clothing. Adam was expecting a guy in black or maybe a couple guys in suits, but this guy was wearing a fluorescent shirt and held a simple iron bar in his hand, not a gun.

Adam grinned, whipping the heat gun at his assailant, now sure that he had the upper hand. But the man never stepped back. He never hesitated. Instead, to Adam's disbelief, the iron bar, that he now realized was some kind of copper tubing used for plumbing, slammed down onto the same hand holding the heat gun. Adam's grip loosened and he felt the heat gun being pulled from his hand. And then, to his complete horror, the blond man didn't cast the gun aside. Instead, he jabbed it into Adam's eye socket, sending searing streams of pain into his skull and down to his toes.

And in the background, Mick Jagger sang on,

I can suck it up
Throw it all at me
I can shrug it off.

NOT THIS TIME, Adam.

CHAPTER SEVENTEEN

The Marine Corps teaches Marines to use "weapons of opportunity." Basically, utilize whatever you can find and overwhelm the enemy with it. I'd used plenty of odd weapons before: branches, bar glasses and even a hardback book. The heat gun was something new. The only downfall? The screams. The guy really wailed, like someone being burned alive. That wouldn't do. The car wash was next to a residential neighborhood, and Mick Jagger wasn't loud enough to cover the sound. So I turned the gun in my hand, and slammed it into his temple. That stopped the screeching and sent him to the floor. Smoke rose from his burning eye socket, a tiny wisp like his eyeball saying its final farewell.

I turned down the music and listened. One minute passed, then five. The guy on the ground hadn't stirred and no one came knocking. No sirens either.

I dragged Mr. One Eye over the wet floor, into the main building and down the short hall to his office. He was twitching a little and I knew that as soon as he woke up the screaming would start again. There was a pile of laundered towels sitting in a basket next to his office door. I grabbed one, wedged the middle in his mouth, and tied the ends around the back of his head. Then I fished around in his pockets and found a keychain. The third key I tried unlocked the office and I pulled him in.

By the time he was fully awake, I had him propped in a chair with his arms and legs bound with electric cord. His one good eye was round like a cue ball, and he was chomping down on the towel in his mouth. I bet the damaged eye hurt, but he'd been the one to make the first move. Try to kill my friend and I'm happy to take your eye.

"Are you ready to talk or do you need some time?" I asked, sitting on the corner of his desk.

He glared at me like he was going to hurt me or something. His bravado was returning and I could see he was probably a real tough guy, at least in his own mind. I had to give him credit. He seemed to be taking the loss of his eye pretty well. He breathed like an angry bull through his nose, but his inhales were slowing as he pulled himself together.

He nodded.

"I'm going to take the towel out of your mouth. If you scream, it goes back on and I grab the heat gun."

He nodded again.

I untied the towel and draped it over his shoulder.

"Good. Now what's your name?" I asked.

"Adam," the man said, hocking a wad of snot and spitting it on the floor.

"What's your last name, Adam?"

"Eplar. Who the fuck are you?"

I ignored the question.

"Adam Eplar. That's a new one. Where are you from, Adam Eplar?"

His eyebrow twitched a little, like he hadn't expected the question.

"I grew up in Boston."

"Where in Boston?"

He named some place I'd never heard of.

"You don't look Irish. I thought only the Irish were from Boston."

He snorted and said, "Then you must be a real moron."

There was something in his voice, the hint of an accent, so faint that if I hadn't been listening for it I might not have noticed.

Just then my phone buzzed. I looked at the screen and shook my head.

"Looks like you've been naughty today, Adam."

"What are you talking about, asshole? I've been on deliveries all day."

I nodded like I believed him, even smiled. The guy was all muscle and no brains.

"You like fires, Adam?"

The text had been from Pastor Walker. He said a neighbor had called to see if he and Anna were okay because of the fire. Their house was gone, the old wood beams consumed by Adam's greedy flames.

His eyebrow twitched again, but he recovered with the same mask of indignation.

"You never told me who you are. You're not a cop, so what the hell do you want?"

He tried to hide his fear, but it was there. I could feel it, and the beast in me licked its lips in anticipation.

"Tell me about Natasha," I said, the comment eliciting the same tell I'd seen twice before.

"I don't know who Natasha is."

"Yes, you do. I hear she bankrolled your little business here and that she sent you to take care of Ed Walker. Does that sound about right?"

I was speculating, but I had to find out about Natasha Varushkin. She was the key to getting Anna back.

Then, to my complete surprise, Adam started laughing. I watched him for a minute, letting the chuckles subside as black liquid oozed from his lost eye.

"Wanna let me in on your joke?" I asked once he'd finished.

"You have no idea who you're dealing—"

My fists cut him off. One, two, three jabs to the nose. Each time his head snapped back like a speed bag. I finished the series off with a sweeping right hook that sent the chair tumbling.

Before he could recover, I had the chair upright again, and my left thumb pressed underneath his good eye. Blood ran freely from his flattened nose, and Adam inhaled deep gulps of air through his mouth like he was going to throw up.

"Tell me where Natasha is," I said evenly.

The ballsy bastard actually smiled. I nodded and smiled back. *You have no idea who* you're *dealing with*, the beast thought with simmering primal intensity.

TEN MINUTES LATER, Adam was a bloody mess. He was lying on his side on the floor, one arm twisted grotesquely to the side. I gave him a chance, had even untied him and let him fight back. Final score? Snake Eyes, one. Adam Eplar, zero.

He'd cracked halfway in, but the beast hammered on. I didn't stop it, watching the beating with a detached curiosity, marveling at the way my alter ego dismantled a professional assassin like a kid on the school playground. Adam was a bully, I could tell by the way he moved, by the way he glared at me. He wasn't used to losing. Tough break for him.

Adam didn't know much, but he'd confirmed his orders to kill Ed Walker. He'd also mentioned something about a high level arrival, an olive branch as he begged me to stop. When I pressed him for details, he couldn't give any. That elicited more pain, more rage from the beast. Too bad for Adam.

Just as his head lay on the ground in resignation, the magic words finally came out of his mouth. An address.

"See, Adam, I told you everyone eventually talks."

He'd bragged about being Special Forces, and as the fight continued, his Russian accent kept slipping out. "I'll never talk," he'd promised.

Wrong again.

I grabbed another towel from outside the office, wiped my face and then my hands. They were covered in Adam's blood. He hadn't landed one punch on me despite being a trained professional. I threw the towel on the floor and told him not to move. I was back a minute later carrying a gas can that I'd found in the back of Adam's van. He was still panting on the floor, his crushed ankle cradled in his only good hand. When he saw the gas can, he started hyperventilating. He shook his head as I poured it over his head, gas running off his face and splashing across the floor.

I walked to the door and pulled something from my pocket. I didn't think twice as I struck the match and flicked it to Adam. He actually tried to catch it, but it did little to stop the fire that flared to life in his hand and then engulfed him completely. By the time I slipped out the back door, the fire alarms inside the car wash were wailing, but Adam's screams were louder.

CHAPTER EIGHTEEN

They sat on the sun deck together, waiting for the sunrise, just as they had each morning for the entire journey. Georgy Varushkin, former Soviet Navy Captain and his faithful steward Vasily. As pale tangerine turned to pink and then a brilliant yellow, they gazed east from where they'd come. Both men knew they would never return to their homeland. To Varushkin, it was a broken land, corrupt and frozen, a shell of its former glory.

He turned away from the sun and looked west, to his new home, to his new life, and to where he would finally be reunited with his family.

———

The night before, Anna's mother had treated her daughter to the fanciest dinner Anna had ever eaten. There was escargot (something she'd only read about), bourbon glazed pork belly, three kinds of pasta, and a tray of desserts that made Anna think of Marie Antoinette.

They talked through dinner and Anna did her best not to

chatter too much. The novelty of hearing her mother's voice still entranced her, like a lullaby she'd longed to hear since childhood.

After dinner, they walked through downtown, always shadowed by her mother's security contingent. When Anna asked about them, her mother explained that people with money needed protection, especially in large cities. Anna had never had any exposure to bodyguards other than the movies she'd watched. She remembered watching Whitney Houston's classic *The Bodyguard* and wondered if the smartly dressed men following them were willing to jump in the path of a bullet for her mother. And then it hit her. Just by being there with her mother, she was being protected, too. Would the bodyguards take a killing blow for her?

The question disturbed her and she didn't bring up the bodyguards again. Mostly her mother asked questions to get a better sense of Anna. While many teenagers might not warm to such questioning, Anna answered freely and from her heart. It was all she'd ever wanted, a mother. While she worried about her father, she was still filled with the Christmas morning glow of a new gift, a life-changing treasure.

They'd walked and talked, much like the way Anna imagined two women strolling down lively Paris streets, commenting on the day's gossip and enjoying each other's company. It was the loveliest evening she could remember.

And things were about to get better. As her mother pulled the covers over her chest the night before, she'd kissed her on the forehead and whispered in her ear. "Tomorrow, you meet your grandfather."

She'd hugged her mother on impulse, the warmth of her rekindled family filling her almost to the bursting point.

As she slept, she dreamed of her mother and an old man with a fuzzy face. Anna couldn't make out his features, but in her dreams he seemed kind, like someone who would sit by a fireplace and read to you into the wee hours. She'd also seen her father as she slept, his face drawn and tired. Her excitement pushed those images away, clearing the puffy smoke-screen to reveal another face, gentle yet wounded, kind yet reserved. His blond hair swayed by some unseen breeze, a smile peeking out from perfect lips. *Daniel. Where is Daniel?*

———

NATASHA WAITED ON THE PIER, flanked by two of her ever-present staff. When she saw her father's face at the top of the ramp, she smiled and even waved; something she hadn't done in years. But as he moved closer, her smile faded. She'd had limited contact with her father, and communication had always been through a well-paid intermediary. Her father had always said he was well. He'd lied. She was shocked to see him wheeled down the ramp, and she was horrified to see his wiry frame.

Georgy Varushkin had been a tall, proud man, a Navy officer others had always looked up to. Now he looked withered and ancient, frail and weary. Despite his appearance, he smiled and she saw his eyes, still bright and strong, as if bragging that even the worst prisons could not take away their sparkle. She returned the smile, but inside she promised to find out who had done this to her father and have them all killed.

She embraced him as soon as his man servant pulled to a stop. Natasha tried not to focus on the bony shoulders her arms wrapped around. She kissed him on the cheek instead, his skin tight like leather. It took every ounce of self control not to wince.

"My Natasha, let me look at you," he said, his voice the same as she remembered. He stroked her hair with a bony hand and grabbed her arm with his other. There were tears in his eyes. She'd never once seen her father cry. "You are more beautiful than I remembered."

Natasha nodded, her voice momentarily unusable. Her aide saved her by saying, "Captain, a car is waiting to take you home."

"Home," her father said dreamily. "Yes, let us go."

He did not release her hand as they moved to the stretch limo, and only surrendered it when his man placed him in the back of the car. Natasha got in on the other side, and slid in next to her father. He grabbed her hand again, and this time she didn't feel like flinching.

They stared at each other for a long moment, and then he asked, "Tell me, when do I get to meet my granddaughter?"

A twinge of jealousy stabbed in her chest, but she said, "Soon, Father. She is waiting."

———

ANNA TOOK turns pacing and sitting. She wanted to look like a proper lady when her grandfather walked in. The problem was all the nervous energy that kept her from sitting still. Instead, she did loops around the expansive foyer, stealing glances out the front window every time she passed.

Finally, when it seemed that an eternity had passed, there was a single honk from outside. A procession streamed in. Anna went to meet the newcomers.

Anna stood at the top of the front steps and waved to her mother when she stepped out of the car. There was something funny in her look, like she was unsure of something. Anna wondered if her mother had been as nervous as she was. *No way*, she thought. *My mom's too cool for that.*

Her next surprise came when the bald guy who'd stepped out of the passenger side door walked to the back of the limo, popped the trunk, and pulled out a wheelchair. Was someone hurt? Was her grandfather hurt?

Anna's heart raced as she watched the man wheel the chair to the opposite side of the limo. He opened the door, bent down, and a moment later Anna saw the silvery white hair of someone being lifted out of the car. The bald man said something to the elderly man, who nodded in response. Anna still couldn't see his face.

She'd been so entranced by the spectacle on the street that she hadn't noticed her mother now stood next to her. She touched Anna on the arm.

"Anna, come inside. I must tell you something."

"But Grandfather..."

"You will see him in a moment. Come."

Anna took one look back and saw four men bending down to take hold of the wheelchair, whose back still faced the brownstone.

"What is it?" Anna asked as soon as they stepped inside.

There was pain in her mother's eyes, sadness. A new thing for Anna.

"Your grandfather is not well," her mother explained.

"Why? What happened?" Anna had so many questions and had to bite her tongue to keep them all from spilling out.

Her mother hesitated. "The people who had your grandfather were not kind. He is much different than the last time I saw him."

Anna's chest tightened. "Is he going to die?" she blurted.

Her mother smiled. "I don't think so. Your grandfather is made of stone and sea. There are few things that can break him."

Anna didn't understand what that meant, but she nodded and turned back to the door. The servants had set the wheelchair down just inside the door, and Anna got her first glimpse of the man with silver hair. She inhaled sharply, taking a tentative step forward. He waited for her, and then nodded for Anna to come closer. She did, taking in every aspect of his shriveled body. But Anna quickly dismissed those things as her eyes came to rest on his. She inhaled again, and to her surprise, so did he. She felt caught, like an invisible magnetic beam had latched on to her and had frozen her body. And yet she felt herself moving, and he opened his arms. A moment later, she was hugging him and he was holding her to his chest.

Her tears ran freely and she felt wet droplets landing on the back of her head. A heart thumped steadily in the chest next to her ear and she listened like it would give her some insight into this man's soul, her grandfather, a man she never knew existed. So when she pulled back and looked into his clear eyes again, eyes that she now realized looked just like hers, a feeling hit her like she'd been touched by a fairy's wand. She knew it with every ounce of her being. She knew it more surely than she'd ever known anything in her life.

This was home. *He* was her home.

CHAPTER NINETEEN

We had the beginnings of a plan. Over coffee in a 24-hour diner the night before, Pastor Walker and I discussed our options. He was more engaged this time, offering suggestions and even poking little holes in my plan. It would've been easy to put him in his place, some of his ideas being plain ludicrous, but I let him talk. With each word he uttered, I saw the flickering bulb of bravery doing its best to come full on. He was trying. I was glad for that.

Our first mission was to recon the area and get a better idea of the security in and around Natasha's home. The location was perfect for what I had in mind. Situated a block off of the Boston Common (Walker informed me that it is the oldest park in the country), any number of joggers and pedestrians would pass by the large brownstone on any given day. It was also right next door to the Massachusetts State House and the State Library. If I'd had more time I might've gone to public records to see what I could find, but my gut told me we didn't have the luxury of an extended surveillance operation. Besides, the intel I'd gathered from the guy at the car wash concerning a new gathering had me worried. The assassin made it sound like a big deal, like some kind of pivotal convergence.

Walker pressed me to allow him to come along, even going so far as to tell me that he was in great shape because he ran a few miles at least four times a week. *Sorry, Pastor, you have no idea what great shape means.* Most people thought that having a killer 5K time made you "fit." I'd seen fat body Marines who could barely finish morning PT carry a wounded buddy over a mile, never complaining despite the shrapnel wound they'd neglected to tell the Corpsman about. Combat fit and civilian fit were two very different things.

Instead of telling him this, I instructed Walker to make a series of purchases that would not only keep him busy, but save me time when I returned. He had his list and a strict warning not to purchase more than three items in each place. I gave him a wad of cash from the stack I'd gotten from an ATM and told him I was going to get a couple hours sleep in our motel room. He finished his apple pie while I headed for the door.

Like a trained animal, I moved off to find what sleep I could. But the growling inside my chest urged me to move out now, to find out what I could, expose some weakness and exploit it. It wasn't hard to ignore the thought; hours of combat operations had instilled the importance of sleep and nutrition. It was strange to think that only days before I'd been on a collision course to wreck my body and silence my mind. Now I needed both if I was going to exact my revenge and save Anna.

———

CLICK.

My eyes snapped open. No alarm clock needed. My body knew the hours just before sunrise well. I snatched up the pile of athletic clothes and the matching running shoes from the pile Walker had left next to my bed in the middle of the night. He was still asleep, snoring lightly as I went to the bathroom and changed.

Two and a half minutes later, I was out the door and headed for the street. It was an easy three mile run to Boston Common, and I took it at an eight minute pace. By the time I arrived at the park, the sun was saying its first hellos, and a light sweat ringed my new t-shirt.

I slowed and jogged over to a wooden bench to stretch my legs. I looked around to make sure the map in my head matched what I was now seeing. There were fewer joggers than expected. Not a problem.

A homeless man shuffled by with his shopping cart full of blankets, and as a gaggle of moms and their jogging strollers pushed by, I stretched and took it all in. It was habit. Just like when you take your first steps into a forest or God-forbid a jungle, you always stop and listen for a while. It enables your senses to get used to the sounds and smells around you. It allows your body to ease into the mugginess or the cold, your instincts slipping from human to animal.

I watched the cars pass by on Beacon Street, the congestion already clogging the city's arteries. Thousands of Bostonians on their way to work, bored and on auto-pilot, completely oblivious to the sniper lurking in their midst.

When enough time had elapsed, I headed for the crosswalk over Beacon Street that dumped me onto Joy Street. I took it slow, not knowing how far from her enclave Anna's mother would spread security. There were no heads in the parked cars I passed, no roving patrols.

Barely a block up on my right was Mount Vernon Place, not really a street but a dead end road that you might consider a blunt cul-de-sac without the rounded end. I passed it, noting the pair of men standing on the top of the stairs of the address I was looking for. They were smoking and chatting, and neither man looked my way as I jogged half a block in the distance.

Two blocks later, I decided to take my chances. I turned around and jumped to the other side of the street. Soon I was approaching the same turn onto Mount Vernon Place. I had a half-ass plan in my head and figured I should give it a shot. I'd only get one, but maybe I'd get lucky.

This time the two guys did turn, but kept talking as I jogged by. I ignored them and kept running. At the end of the short road was the official looking state building, and I stopped in supposed confusion. I turned, looked back the way I'd come, then whirled around, looking for a sign or a familiar landmark.

I huffed in frustration, still looking around. My eyes settled on the two guys guarding 7 Mount Vernon Place, the enemy's lair. I jogged back their way and waved a greeting, trying to look embarrassed.

Neither man waved back, but they leveled me with their best "What the fuck do you want?" gaze. I ignored the looks like some naive tourist and said, "Hey, I'm supposed to be meeting a friend at Ashburton Park. Can you tell me how to get there?"

I jogged in place and waited for a reply. Finally, after a look passed between them, one of the guys said, "Keep going that way," he pointed to where I'd turned around a moment earlier, "and skirt around the big building. On the opposite side you'll see the park."

"Great, thanks," I said, nodding to each man. As they turned back to their conversation, I did a quick scan of the windows on the second and third levels. My scan stopped on a pair of ice blue eyes staring down at me from the middle window on the third floor. Anna.

I tried to look away, but couldn't. The two guys noticed and one of them said, "Hey, keep moving okay?"

I shook my head like an idiot. "Sorry, I just love old architecture," I said in a way of an apology.

I waved to them again, and shot one more glance up to the third floor. Anna was staring at me and she put up one hand in a silent greeting. I blinked twice and headed away, my heart thudding in rhythm with my feet pounding on the pavement. She hadn't looked in pain. Truthfully, she looked happy.

That made my mind blare a warning, something I hadn't considered before, or maybe I didn't want to believe. What if she told her mother about me, and what if she told her mother that she'd just seen me again?

CHAPTER TWENTY

"Come in," came the quiet call in response to Vasily's knock on Anna's door. The bald Russian opened the door to its full width and pushed his master into the room.

"Thank you, Vasily," Georgy Varushkin said.

Vasily nodded, and left the room.

Anna was sitting on the window ledge, staring at him with unabashed curiosity. They'd had little time to get acquainted the night before. The gaggle of doctors Natasha had waiting were quick to get him into their hastily made examination room.

So as they'd asked questions, taken vials of blood and probed his entire body, Varushkin went along with the show, polite and uncomplaining. As the physicians and their assistants went about their business, he replayed the greeting with his granddaughter over and over again in his mind. It was one of the few benefits of his incarceration, the ability to recall certain memories in vivid detail, as if he were experiencing them again.

Ah, and this memory was the sweetest he could ever recall. Something had happened when he saw Anna. She had his eyes, the Varushkin eyes his mother said could cut through stone with their intensity.

But there was only love and curiosity in Anna's eyes, like a flower just coming into bloom. It was overpowering to the weakened Varushkin, and it took his nearly empty reserve of strength to only let out a few tears instead of the uncontrollable sobs that howled to be unleashed. Later, as he'd pondered the introduction, Georgy would have explained the feeling as being similar to an electric shock. In his years of service, he'd been shocked on one occasion. The ailing Soviet fleet had sagged under the weight of political pressure and the constant American presence. Despite the proactive measures of commanders like Varushkin, supplies were limited, and ships were often undermanned and less than well-kept. This resulted in accidents, mishaps that only years before could have been prevented.

On one occasion, an electrical wire had somehow become frayed from a line running alongside a ladder well. It just so happened that not long after, Varushkin, on his way to the bowels of his ship, had grasped the metal railing that was now charged with enough electric current to hold him in place for a moment, and then his body weight dropped him back. There was not much pain, but the captain could never shake that feeling of being held in place, and until the night before, he'd never felt it again.

When he had lain in bed thinking more of that moment, he knew in his heart it was some sort of sign, like the stars were aligning and Anna was the final missing piece. It stirred a youthful excitement in him, and kept him from sleep. He'd woken Vasily at first light, and waited as long as he could to visit Anna. It was good to see that she might feel the same way.

"I could not sleep," he said.

"Me neither."

"Was there a reason?"

She smiled. Ah, that smile. "I kept thinking of you, and I wanted to know that you were okay."

"You mean because of the doctors?"

She nodded.

He nodded back.

"I'm sure they will return with the following prognosis: Mr. Varushkin is malnourished, severely underweight, infested with this and that parasite, and we recommend a trip to the dentist."

Anna giggled. He didn't want to scare her. There was most certainly more wrong with him, but at least he didn't feel like he was dying. For some reason, he'd always known that he would have a premonition before his death. He'd thought his time in prison would have elicited such a feeling, but it never had, not in five years.

"How do you feel?" Anna asked.

He shrugged. "I have been better, but I am sure that with the help of the doctors, I will be fat in no time. Enough about me, please, I want to hear all about you, Anna." He held out his hand, and she grabbed it. Her hand was soft and clean where his was wrinkled and dry. An old prisoner's hand.

"Well," she started, "I'm fifteen. I guess you can say I'm pretty smart. I love to read and I love music. Oh, and I want to travel around the world!"

He couldn't help but smile. Her exuberance filled him with warmth and made the pain in his body subside.

"And where would you like to travel, Anna? Paris? London?"

Her eyes lit up like he'd read her mind. "Yes! Oh, and I want to go to Russia, to see where our family is from."

The cold that enveloped him felt like a wraith had entered the room and cast its shawl across his body. He shivered, momentarily losing his grip on Anna's hand.

"I'm sorry, Poppa, did I say something wrong?" Anna asked, taking his hand again and stepping closer.

He hadn't realized his eyes had closed. He opened them and shook his head.

"I am fine. It must be the medicine they gave me."

She did not believe him, but she didn't push.

"Poppa?" he asked.

Anna blushed, the possible transgression already forgotten.

"I'm sorry. Is it okay if I call you that?"

"I would be honored, Anna," he said, the warmth returning to his body.

They sat there for a long moment, both wearing contented smiles, not saying anything, as if to do so would break the spell in the room, their private domain.

"I'm so glad you're here, Poppa," Anna said at last, taking his hand in both of hers. "I wish we could have met before."

He nodded knowingly and said, "I have found that it is best not to live with regret. It is better to look to the future and create a joy that will outshine the shadows of our past."

Her mouth twisted in a funny smile.

"Do you always talk that way, Poppa?"

Varushkin coughed out a laugh. "Maybe it has been too long since I've had a proper conversation. Perhaps you can help me sound less...grandiose?"

Anna nodded and they both grinned.

He didn't know the whole story yet, didn't know how Anna had come back into Natasha's home, but he would get it soon. There was much to discuss in the coming days. His daughter seemed to have things well in hand. Like an old general being called out of retirement, he had to be careful how he moved back into the arena. Five years could change many things. He had changed, and from what he'd seen of Natasha, so had she. He was glad to see she'd turned her life around. From the occasional reports he'd received while behind bars, everything indicated she had conducted herself in a manner befitting his command style. It would be good to see it firsthand.

For now he put those thoughts out of his mind as he focused on the most important thing in that moment, his granddaughter. There was so much he wanted to know, and yet, where to start? *Simple. Start simple*, he told himself.

"So, tell me, what did you see looking out the window this morning?" He had a new fascination with windows. It was only natural considering the rare minutes he'd been gifted to gaze out the small portals in his prison stops. But the innocent question did not elicit what he expected. Instead of answering, Anna hesitated and even looked away. "I'm sorry, Anna," he was quick to add. "Did I say something wrong?"

She shook her head, still looking away.

"Then what is it, child?"

Anna let go of his hand and walked back to the window. She looked down at the street and even touched the pane of glass. With what? Longing?

"I thought I saw a friend," she said, tracing a finger along the edge of the window.

"Who, Anna? Who did you see?"

"I don't think I should say." She was still staring out the window. What was it in her tone that made him worry?

"Anna, look at me please."

She turned and met his eyes.

"Anna, if I have learned one important lesson in my life, it is that you should never keep secrets from the ones you love most."

She perked up a bit at that, and asked, "What if the secret protects a friend?"

He grunted his understanding.

"That must be a very good friend to need such a secret."

"It is," Anna whispered.

"And who is this friend?"

Anna exhaled softly. "Do you promise not to tell anyone, unless I say it's okay?"

"I do. Have you told your mother?"

Anna shook her head, embarrassed.

Varushkin pursed his lips, more questions coming to mind.

"Very well. I will not tell your secret to anyone unless you give me your permission."

Anna nodded and marched forward, her hand extended. They shook like two CEOs coming to an agreement.

"Deal," she said.

"Deal," he repeated. "Now, tell me who your friend is."

Anna's eyes lit up, and she said, "His name is Daniel."

"And who is Daniel?"

Her body was relaxed now.

"Daniel was a Marine, or, is a Marine. You know, they always say once a Marine always a Marine."

Varushkin nodded.

"And this Daniel, how is it that you came to know him?"

"He was staying on our farm in Maine, with me and my dad."

It was the first he'd heard of Anna's father. He'd only met the man once, when Natasha had been in the midst of her drug-filled adventure. He'd seemed like a nice man who had wanted to be a preacher if he remembered correctly. The only reason Varushkin had consented to allow Anna to go with her father was that the young man's background had been clean, except for his tryst with Natasha, and he'd been convincing in his court plea to keep the child.

"And where is your father now?"

Anna's face darkened.

"Something happened," she said, her voice low again, like she was to blame.

"What happened, Anna? Tell me what happened with your father."

Anna nodded absently and began to tell the tale.

"For as long as I can remember, my dad wanted to start a church. It was hard to do it without a lot of money, so one day my dad found some people who said they could help. I think that's when the trouble started."

CHAPTER TWENTY-ONE

Her body felt the rocking rhythm, but her mind was elsewhere, pondering contingencies and calculating returns. Natasha's world was all about control. Her therapist said it was her only way of coping with the world around her. Natasha knew what that meant: Lose control and the downward spiral began again.

She'd had enough of failure. Every time she'd relapsed, Natasha told herself it wasn't her fault, that it was her father or her dead mother. Sometimes it was her DNA and the persistent tug she could never seem to shake.

And then she'd met her last therapist, a cold man with dead eyes who'd taken one look at her and diagnosed everything he believed to be wrong with her. That woke Natasha. There were no tissue boxes or comfy chairs in the man's office. He was all business and told her in that first meeting that he reserved the right to fire her, not the other way around.

She'd agreed to his stringent terms and plunged headlong into therapy. Cut by cut she carved her life down to its most important parts. Precisely one year into her therapy, though at times she would have described it as more of an indentured servitude, her doctor asked Natasha what she wanted out of life.

"Now that you've risen above much of your tainted life, I'm sure your vision has cleared. Tell me, Ms. Varushkin, where do you see yourself in five, ten, twenty years?"

She'd been so focused on getting better that thoughts of the future seemed as foreign as a butterfly in a sweatshop. He saw her hesitation and gave her the week to think about it, again with the same caveat.

"Come with your answer, or see yourself to the door."

It was one of the hardest, most thought-provoking weeks of her life. She spent many hours running on a treadmill or power-walking around the city, winding in and around places known and unknown, until she couldn't remember where she was.

The answer came late one night after a hurried call from her father. The elder Varushkin was in Russia for business, shoring up a land deal that could net many millions. He made no mention of it during his call.

"Natasha, the military police have come for me. They are taking me in for questioning. I will call when I can."

The line went dead and she scrambled to find information. No one she called could tell her anything. She was helpless again, floundering without the aid of her father. And that was when it happened, like a heavy leather page turning to the next, a fight against gravity.

Her mind cleared and she knew what she wanted.

She never went back to her therapist because she knew it was what he wanted. If she truly had found her calling, she didn't need him anymore. No, everything was clear now. She had to take control of her father's interests, she had to save him, she had to rise to her new calling and run her father's organization.

It started slowly, and some of the men tried to get in her way. She found clever ways of disposing of their services, and soon she was in complete control. Her father's contacts knew they had no choice but to trust her. After all, she held their money and their futures. Five years of working, slaving, overpowering, and now she was so close. The final culmination of the plans that would ensure her future, solidify her control.

But little things were brewing worry in her subconscious. Her father was home, but he was weak and she swore he looked at her differently. Her daughter was home, but Natasha had a hard time looking at Anna and not feeling a twinge of jealousy for Anna's youth and beauty, the innocent inquisitiveness in her eyes. Then there was the upcoming gathering. Five years in the making, it should be the crowning achievement of her toils.

And yet she worried, a sliver of control lost. Why couldn't she shake it?

A bead of sweat ran off her neck, between her breasts and landed on her personal trainer's chiseled stomach. He was looking up at her with rapt attention, moving with her, obviously trying to last longer. But when her mind came back to the task at hand, she grabbed a handful of his hair and moved faster. He finished in seconds.

"Get your clothes on," she said, sliding off of him and walking naked to the bathroom. "I hope you can do better when we get to the gym."

———

THE GYM HELPED MORE than the screwing, and by the time she arrived back at the brownstone, she was showered and clear-headed. The cook had a plain omelet waiting in her room, and she devoured it as she changed.

She was surprised that Anna hadn't stopped in. Since

arriving, the teenager seemed to have an uncanny knack for knowing when her mother was about. Maybe she was with her grandfather. The thought made Natasha wince, the dark clouds from the morning threatening to dampen her mood.

When she went to the kitchen to find a glass of water, the cook told her that Mr. Varushkin was in the sunroom reading. She found him staring out the window, the sunshine caressing his sallow face. He turned when she entered, and returned her embrace with an added kiss.

"I'm sorry I missed breakfast," she said quickly, chiding herself immediately. She wasn't a child anymore. Why did he make her feel that way?

"I had time to talk to Anna," he said, still holding her hand. Something in his voice made her shiver.

"How is Anna this morning?" she said, releasing his hand and refilling her glass with the pitcher of orange juice on the side table.

"She is confused."

"Oh?" Natasha's heartbeat quickened.

"She worries about her father."

"Well she shouldn't. I'm sure he's just fine." She avoided his gaze, focusing instead on the pile of pastries next to the orange juice, a necessary distraction at the moment.

"Have you been in contact with him?"

"Not since Anna got here."

"Why is that?"

"Anna felt uncomfortable, so I thought I should give her some time."

"And this thing about the girls?"

She turned to face him. His face hadn't changed. She'd never been able to read him. He had the unnerving ability to remain placid despite the situation. It angered her that the gift had not been passed down to her.

Natasha wanted to lie, wanted to tell her father the same

story she'd told Anna, that the girls were safely in the hands of the authorities. But he would know she was lying, he always had.

"What do you want me to tell you, Father?"

"The truth, Natasha."

She exhaled and said, "The girls are safe."

"Where are they?"

"They are with the gentlemen who requested them."

Natasha saw her father's hand tense and then release.

"You sold them," he said flatly.

She nodded, unapologetic.

"Why?" he asked. "I was told—"

"You were gone, Father. You left, remember? Everything I did was to make you proud, to prepare for your return. It is because of me that you are here. It is because of me that you have something to come back to." It was all true. She'd always wanted to make her father proud, to stand next to him as they ascended into a new world of security and freedom.

"But the girls. Why the girls?"

Her glare turned into a hard laugh.

"Do you know how much those girls made us? Millions. Millions, Father. And that was only one small shipment!"

Now his eyes went wide. Her exclamation was supposed to elicit pride in him. All she saw was horror. She rushed to explain.

"We've divested every other illegal interest we had. Our real estate holdings have doubled each year. The complex in Wyoming is ready, and The Pension is invested in so many businesses that only a nuclear war could destroy it. We even started a venture capital firm to find and invest in new technologies. Father, this is what we dreamed of. This is our future, and it is wonderful to behold."

She was holding her hands out wide, demonstrating what she'd built while he was away. She looked to him for approval, for some sign that he understood. He shook his head and looked away instead.

"It is my fault. I should have been more clear. When we took what we did, the plan was always to get out of the criminal world. Can you not see how dangerous this is? Can you not see how one word from a disloyal employee could bring the entire American government down on our family?" He kept shaking his head like a homeless man with a twitch.

"Nobody will find out. We've made the transactions seamless and invisible."

"And that's why your daughter knows about this?"

Natasha froze. He did not understand and never would. Her visage went cool.

"That was a mistake, a mistake that has been remedied."

Georgy Varushkin looked up at his only daughter and said, "You were right. You have done well, better than I ever could have asked. But hear me now, as of today, The Pension no longer traffics anything. We have put illegal dealing behind us. It was the promise I made to our investors, to our brothers. Do you understand me, Natasha?"

She stared at him for an extended moment. His eyes were so blue, like the deep cuts of a glacier. But where she'd once seen strength and determination, she now saw weakness and a slow death.

Despite her thoughts, Natasha nodded and said, "I will do as you say, Father."

She bent down and kissed him on the cheek. He held her close and she tried not to move. When he let go and looked up at her, it took every ounce of hard-won control to smile and nod. He returned the smile and she left the room.

As soon as she was in the office, she shut the French doors and picked up the phone on the desk. The call picked up after the second ring with a gruff, "Yes?"

"We need to talk," Natasha said, scraping a nail on the

back of her hand, watching as the blood rushed to the surface and left a white trail when it disappeared. "I'll see you in an hour."

She replaced the phone in the cradle. Things would move quickly now. She hadn't heard from Adam Eplar yet, but the car wash usually kept him busy in the mornings, and it had probably been a long night. He would call when he had time. He'd never failed her before.

With her ex-husband out of the way, the trail from Old Orchard Beach was cut off. Finding an alternate route would be easy. Despite what her father had said, she had no intention of halting their trafficking operations. They were too lucrative and had turned into one of her power centers. Men wanted power, and usually they wanted it over women. With the girls shipped in from Ukraine, Natasha had quietly wrested that power from them, even establishing a vibrant spy network that funneled all sorts of interesting tidbits into her organization. She had no intention of letting that power go. If her father couldn't live with that, she could live without him. After all, she was used to it after the last five years.

CHAPTER TWENTY-TWO

S*uicide mission.*

The words echoed in my head until I finally shook them away. Pastor Walker looked up from where he'd been staring at his hands. I assumed he'd been praying. He'd done a lot of that since coming to Boston. Who knew if it worked, but it seemed to make him feel better, looser and more apt to help.

"What is it?" he asked.

I shook my head again, the vision of Anna's eyes still splitting me right down the middle. Again two sides of a coin. Decisions. I was used to being a loner. Now all I could think about was ways I could get in and out with Anna. The Marine in me said to look at other options, to ignore my beast and look at the situation objectively.

"We can't do this alone," I said, thinking out loud now, as if saying the words might propel me back to firm reality.

Walker tensed. We'd talked about bringing in the authorities and letting them handle the Varushkins. The talk hadn't gone far. We knew what that would mean. Even if the police or the FBI cracked the Russian clan, there were still Anna and now her father to consider. Anna would probably get snatched up by social services, and I wasn't a big enough prick to let the pastor get nabbed for something his ex-wife set him up for, no matter how stupid he'd been.

No, there had to be another way, a way to skirt the law and come out on the other side. I saw the beginnings of a path lined by concertina wire. Everything else was a blur, like I just had to take the first steps and see what happened next.

My mind fluttered back to the room, to the concerned look on the pastor's face, to the cracked tiles in the motel bathroom, to faded paintings of some fictional beach. I stared at the picture for a long time, willing the answer to come, begging it to be seen. Nothing.

"What about your friends from the Marine Corps?" Walker asked. "Is there anyone you could call?"

There were plenty of people I *could* call, but none that I wanted to call. I'd made a clean break, put all that behind me. No one knew how to find me now. No one knew where...

I stopped cold, the faded memory bursting like a bubble in my head.

"Rex," I said, surprised when the name slipped out.

"Who?"

I closed my eyes and thought about the last time I'd talked to Rex Hazard. He'd been one of my STA (Surveillance and Target Acquisition) Platoon Commanders. That's where Marine snipers usually come from, property of Marine battalions or regiments. 1st Lt. Hazard was different than the rest. Most of those lieutenants came in wanting to be snipers themselves. Who could blame them? They were infantry officers by trade and intelligence officers by training. Hazard told me a lot of his fellow Ground Intelligence officers got stuck in S-2, the battalion's intel shop. The lucky ones got platoons like their infantry officer brethren. He'd almost missed his chance, had somehow convinced someone high up to let him stay on even though he'd soon pick up captain.

1st Lt. Hazard came to STA as a veteran intelligence officer, having been part of the planning for untold operations during the invasion of Iraq. He was smart and he listened. He knew the value of Marine snipers like me, knew how to employ us and how to best support us. Sometimes he asked to come along, but even when he did, he left us to our tasks, even hauling our chow and extra ammo like some boot PFC.

When he took over command, Hazard already knew who I was. I'd met him on a couple occasions. I didn't know him though.

Our first stint in Afghanistan changed that. It was a long range insertion and he came along for the ride. The rest of our teams had been tasked to companies, but they liked to put me and my spotter deep in Indian country. We knew how to stay hidden, and I could always be counted on to take the toughest shots. That's not bragging. It's just how it was.

To make a long story short, we got unlucky. The place we picked to setup camp ended up being a favored mating place for wild dogs. They don't put that kind of stuff on maps. Not an hour after the helo put the three of us on the ground, the yelping started. The yelps turned to barks when the mangy dogs realized we were there.

Once again, luck went the other way. As so often happens, someone got curious. They must've heard the dogs and a band of armed guys headed our way. It was dark, but I could see them clearly through my scope. We radioed higher to see if they knew who the guys were, but that turned up jack and shit. We asked for a helo, but were told to lay low or get to a new location. The quickest timeframe they could get to us was three hours.

Lt. Hazard let me make the call. The guys with guns were close, and I could see there were more coming. Either they thought they'd have some sport with the wailing mutts, or they thought there was something else going on. I still put my money on the first.

We got to our feet and I told Hazard to make for the hills. We didn't get fifty feet before the firing started. That first volley hit the lieutenant, and he stumbled in the dirt.

I had no choice at that point. I pushed Hazard to the ground and told my spotter to get down too. By the time I was on the ground I'd already taken out two. They couldn't see us down low, so the shooting was easy. Turned out they were the bad guys we were supposed to be watching the next day, but they'd arrived earlier than expected. Gotta love shitty intel. We got out after the bad guys took heavy casualties and turned tail.

After that, Hazard and I were pretty close. When he was getting out of the Corps, he invited me to the Officers Club where they were giving him his farewell. He pissed off a few officers by doing that, and probably pissed off the rest when he invited me up on the makeshift stage and told everyone in attendance that he owed Sgt. Briggs his life, and that "good ol' Snake Eyes" was the best Marine he'd ever served with.

I really never thought about him again until he tracked me down almost a year before rolling into Old Orchard Beach, Maine. He said he was with the FBI now. He was building a team, and I was his number one draft pick.

I let him down easy, giving him some line about never working for the government again. He gave me his number and said to keep in touch. I never did, but I still had his number.

Pastor Walker watched as I placed the call on the motel room phone. I smiled when I heard Rex Hazard's familiar voice, a voice from my past, a voice springing a well of distant memories.

"Special Agent Hazard," he answered.

"Rex, it's Daniel."

"Snake Eyes?"

"Yeah."

"Well, holy fucking shit, Marine. Where the fuck are you?"

I forgot to mention that Hazard had one of the filthiest mouths I'd ever heard, and that included every gunnery sergeant I'd served with.

"I'm in Boston. Are you still in New York City?"

"Yeah, just outside. What's going on, man?"

I hesitated. His exuberance surprised me, made me remember that some people thought I was a hero, some kind of savior. I wasn't, but they still thought it.

"I need your help."

His voice went serious, like I remembered. "Name it."

"How much do you know about the Russian mob?"

"More than some, but less than others."

I grunted.

"Let's start with information."

"What do you need?" he asked, back in battle mode.

"I need you to find out about a woman named Varushkin, Natasha Varushkin."

I could hear keyboard clicking on his end.

"Okay, can you give me an hour?"

"The quicker the better, Rex."

"Roger. Hold tight. Hazard, out."

The line went dead.

"FBI?" Walker asked nervously.

I nodded.

"An old friend from the Corps. Good man."

Walker looked down at his hands again and went back to his praying.

I didn't pray, but I did hope that Hazard could dig up something that might help. My life wasn't much, and yet, some part of me still wanted to keep it. If I could get in and out alive, I'd do that. If worst came to worst, I'd give it away just to burn the whole Varushkin family to the ground and see Anna safe.

I smiled at the thought. Yeah. That's exactly what needed to happen. The world didn't have enough matches for what I planned to do to Natasha Varushkin.

CHAPTER TWENTY-THREE

Special Agent Rex Hazard's cursor flew across the computer screen, clicking and scrolling as his eyes followed. The phone call was a surprise. He hadn't seen Sergeant Briggs in years, the last time was the hazy farewell at the O-Club at Lejeune. Despite the time apart, not a day went by that he didn't think of the sniper, wondering where he was, hoping he would find his way back to civilization.

Under the authority he'd been given to recruit team members, Hazard had placed a simple tracking system on the trail of Daniel Briggs. Whenever he made a withdrawal, Hazard knew. If Briggs was ever to leave the country, Hazard would know. Up to this point, good ol' Snake Eyes had followed a meandering path, a vagabond's journey through the south and now up the east coast. Former Marine Captain Rex Hazard noted the passage and imagined what the famed sniper was up to.

He'd known Briggs as an honest and reserved sniper who avoided praise and could always be counted upon. Simply put, Daniel Briggs was one of the best snipers the Marine Corps had ever trained. It was one of the reasons Capt. Hazard had put him up for the Medal of Honor. Well, that and what he'd done in Afghanistan. Briggs was never the same after that, and the Marine Corps had even contacted Hazard to see if they knew of the Marine's whereabouts. He always knew, but he never told. If Snake Eyes needed his space, Hazard would let him have it. There were too many boys who came home to a confusing world filled with citizens who didn't quite get what troops did, even though many tried.

Now it was Hazard's turn to give back, not only for Briggs saving his life, but for the debt he'd paid for his country, for the sacrifice, for the pain.

Hazard perused the files on Natasha Varushkin. There was her entry visa and a corresponding Russian passport photo. Even as a teen she was striking, a real knockout. As the years passed on the screen, Natasha aged with the grace of a perfectly crafted wine. But her personal actions soon contradicted the beauty of the pixels.

She was first arrested in college for underage consumption. Not that big a deal. The next arrest was for possession of marijuana, then another. The three disorderly conducts came next, and then the assault on a male companion. Even in her mug shot Varushkin looked poised and beautiful.

Then it all stopped. Almost five years ago exactly, the arrests ceased and so did normal activities like bank card use, driver's license scans and international travel.

"That's strange," Hazard said to himself. He double checked, and sure enough, Natasha Varushkin had ceased to exist on the official United States radar. That didn't mean records weren't available, but he sure as hell couldn't access them.

Rather than run straight to his boss and ask for assistance with a higher level query (the investigation wasn't exactly official, after all), Special Agent Hazard went with another option: next of kin.

Two brothers, Igor and Frederick. Both dead. The only living relative was her father, Georgy Varushkin. When Hazard tried to access the elder Varushkin's file, nothing showed.

"Fuck."

With a reluctance bred from years of independent action, Special Agent Hazard picked up the phone and dialed his boss. The secretary picked up.

"Hey, Sara, is the old man in?"

"He just got back, hold one."

Hazard waited until his boss came on.

"Rex?"

"Yes, sir."

"Oh crap. If you're calling me sir, there must be something you want."

Ten years Hazard's senior, his boss was a good guy. He was another Marine who'd made it as far up the FBI totem pole as he was going to get. He knew it, but didn't let it get in the way of the job or training his men.

"I need access to a file. Wait, make that two," Hazard added, remembering the ghost file on the dad.

"Send me what you've got and I'll run a search."

"Thanks, boss."

"Yeah, yeah. The next time we play golf you owe me five strokes."

"You got it."

Hazard hung up the phone and smiled. His boss would need more than five strokes to beat him. Even though the senior agent played ten times as much as him, he just couldn't overcome the years of ingrained repetition that Hazard stored in his body from playing on his college golf team. It came in handy when he wanted to show some snobby Ivy Leaguer that a lowly Marine from Columbus, Ohio could beat him whenever he wanted.

As he waited, Hazard replayed the conversation with Briggs. The guy had the same intensity he remembered, not much fluff in his tone. *Focused*, thought Hazard. That's what Briggs was. Like a panther stalking its prey, Snake Eyes never let go.

That worried the thirty-something FBI agent. What the hell was the sniper doing snooping on the Russian mob? The Varushkin file hadn't said anything about organized crime, but the FBI didn't know everything. Even in a post-9-11 world, there were still plenty of secrets hidden in plain sight.

As he organized his thoughts for the return call to Briggs, his phone rang.

"Hazard."

"Why did you say you wanted these files?" his boss asked.

Oh shit.

"I didn't, sorry."

"So tell me."

He'd been vague for a reason, but he didn't want to lie.

"I got a tip on some possible Russian mob activity up in Boston. May have ties to Manhattan."

Silence on the other end. Then his boss said, "Dead end on Natasha Varushkin. Looks like she cleaned up her act and somehow stayed under the radar."

"And the dad?"

Another pause and more silence.

"Where'd you get the tip from, Rex?" his boss asked.

"One of my Marines."

"You mean from your time in."

"Yeah."

"And what is he doing digging up stuff on the mob?"

"Honestly, boss, I don't know."

An even longer pause. *Fuck, he's gonna kill me.*

"One more question, Rex, and you better be on the level, you hear me?"

"Yes, sir," Hazard answered hopefully.

"Why are you helping this guy?"

"The truth?"

"The truth."

Hazard exhaled and then said, "He saved my life. The guy's right up there with fucking Dan Daly and Chesty Puller."

"Can you tell me who he is?"

"Over a beer, yeah."

Hazard heard a grunt, his boss's way of giving in.

"Okay. Here's the deal. The file on the father is a dead end too."

"But I thought you—"

"Will you shut your pup mouth, Marine?"

"Sorry," Hazard said.

"Jesus. If I'd known you were going to be such a pain in the ass I never would have recommended you for that promotion." But there was mutual affection there. He'd handpicked Hazard for the job and they both knew it. Not many people could be trusted to do what Hazard's experimental unit did. "Look, when I said it was a dead end, I meant it's a dead end for us. I can't get access, get it?"

Hazard understood. Georgy Varushkin was a target for a very important government agency, and maybe more than one.

"So is that it? Should I drop it?" Hazard asked.

His boss chuckled.

"If you had another boss, probably. Look, what did your sergeant instructors tell you to do when you didn't know something?"

There weren't many proscribed responses to the stern instructor staff at Officer Candidate School at Quantico. While similar to enlisted boot camp, there were certain differences in the way officer candidates address the screaming enlisted men who commanded them around the clock. Instead of drill instructor you said sergeant instructor. "Yes, sergeant instructor," and, "No, sergeant instructor," were the most common responses to questions. In the early days of summer training, another oft repeated response was, "This candidate does not know, but will find out, sergeant instructor."

That's what his boss was getting to.

He went on, "I'm sure you've got plenty of friends in our fellow alphabet organizations, Rex. Why don't you see if you can contact them while you saddle up with some of your boys. Sounds like your Marine could use the help."

Hazard grinned. He'd be sad to see the old man go.

"Thanks, boss."

He ended the call and speed dialed another. His assistant team leader picked up before the second ring.

"What's up?"

"You, me, and your choice of four men are heading up to Boston. Casual civilian attire. Heavy weapons on standby."

"You got it. When do we leave?"

Hazard looked at his watch.

"Thirty minutes. See if you can wrangle a helo."

"No problem. The flyboys haven't had much to do this week."

Hazard's next call was to Briggs. He kept it short, informing the Marine that they'd be there in the next couple of hours.

"Thanks," was Briggs's simple reply.

For the second time that day, Hazard thought about what could make Snake Eyes (of all the fucking people in the world) ask for help. Something must really be fucked in Boston to ring the silent alarm bell.

As Hazard placed his last call to another Marine buddy who'd landed in the shady underworld of CIA operations, the former STA platoon commander steeled himself for the coming action. If Briggs was onto something, it would undoubtedly be something big. Hazard thought back to the last time he'd been with Briggs in the field, and the fact that he almost hadn't come home. That's how it was with the sniper. The Marine was a magnet for action, like the world was trying to throw everything it could at him and still he kept coming out on top. Hazard knew neither he nor any other man was quite so lucky, and he wondered why. He shrugged off the worry as his old friend came on the line.

"Julian, you got a minute to talk?"

CHAPTER TWENTY-FOUR

Natasha accepted the lingering hug from the man she'd come to see, but it took every ounce of self control she had not to cringe. Her host finally held her at arm's length and said, "You get more lovely every time I see you."

She smiled politely at the man she knew simply as Joe. Physically, the only things that made him halfway remarkable were his flat nose and protruding belly. The rest of him wasn't fat, but his stomach distended like some starving child in Africa.

"It is good to see you, Joe," she said, accepting the added peck on either cheek.

"It is not every day that I get to see such beauty," Joe continued, waving her toward the chairs nestled in the corner of the tiny office.

She chuckled and said, "If what I've heard is true, you have a steady stream of beauty flowing through your arms."

He shrugged, but was in no way embarrassed. It was true. The Russian immigrant was rarely seen without at least four stunningly beautiful women. Natasha knew this because some of those very women had come from her Ukrainian supply chain.

"So, what is it that brings you to my humble office?" Joe asked, settling in his favored leather armchair.

Natasha knew she was walking into mined territory; any wrong step could mean disaster. Despite how he might look, Joe ran one of the largest illicit Russian organizations in Boston, and was even making headway into the jewel of the east, New York City.

"I think it may be time for us to join forces," Natasha said, hating to say the words even as they came out of her mouth.

Joe's eyebrows shot up.

"Please tell me my charms have finally rubbed off on you," he replied.

The man was always thinking with his penis.

"Business, Joe, I was talking about business."

He put on his best wounded look, but Natasha knew it was a ruse. Joe had enough tail to chase. Nabbing her would only be a temporary bonus.

"Business?" Joe asked, his tone now level, the playfulness gone. "Wasn't it you who told me our business would strictly be what it had been?"

It was true. Up until that point, Natasha had only supplied Joe's organization with women. She procured the best and he paid top dollar. It was a good business relationship, lucrative for both sides. But after the conversation with her father, Natasha needed backing. If she was going to pull off her plan, she would need the help of one of the Varushkins's original rivals. It was a necessary evil given the tight timeline.

Natasha leaned forward, knowing she was giving Joe a perfect view of her perfect breasts. She smiled and said, "Things have changed."

Joe rubbed his hands together, and Natasha counted no less than three glances down the front of her blouse.

"You know I have always desired a more...intimate business relationship with you, Natasha. So tell me, how do you envision the consummation of this new arrangement?"

Natasha smiled and said, "I need you to kill my father."

———

THE NEWS from Rex was a mixed bag. It would be nice to have some backup, but that was only if things got really bad. He was clear on that point.

"If shit hits the fan, like the OK Corral on the streets of Boston, we'll jump in. But if you keep it contained, we stay out."

That was fine with me. There'd been big messes in the past, but I wasn't planning on that this time. A quick in and out would be a good place to start. Picking up some intel to pass on to Rex would be a bonus, but Anna was my top priority.

I didn't tell Rex about my plans for Anna's mother. He didn't need to know. That might put him in an awkward position, and someone with the FBI didn't need that kind of heat. Better to tear the place up and let Rex "independently" uncover the plot. My name would never be mentioned.

When Rex's team made their first pass, he called to tell me that their scans picked up at least twenty warm bodies inside the Varushkin brownstone.

"We'll make another run in thirty minutes," he'd said.

Twenty people. One of them was Anna and some had to be servants or maids. Even if five were house staff that still left fourteen possible enemies with guns. Things could get ugly, and fast.

Ideas rolled around in my head. Sure I could break in, but then what? By the time I reached Anna, the whole house would know someone was there. No, that wouldn't work. They make it look easy in the movies. In the real world, there are alarms (which I could not disarm) and there are people. Real security personnel, like those employed by the Varushkins, wouldn't be as stupid as those movie characters, where the actors probably get paid a hundred bucks for dying quickly.

I needed something sure, something that would minimize the risk to Anna. More ideas came and went as I shuffled them into my mind's trash bin. There had to be something, and that something came soon after. The phone rang. It was Rex.

"Hey, I've got one more friend on board," he said.

"Oh?"

"Yeah, another dumb grunt who owes me some favors."

"What's his specialty?" I asked.

Rex snorted. "Short of a fucking airstrike, he can probably get it done."

My mind whirred with the possibilities. The idea was to keep the thing contained, to give me a big enough window to retrieve Anna. Rex was telling me the genie was in town and he was about to grant me one wish.

"Okay," I said. "Here's what I'm gonna need."

———

"Sure. Yeah, that shouldn't be a problem."

Julian Fog chewed on a toothpick as he listened to Rex Hazard and then hung up the phone. He'd worked for Hazard in the Corps as a Corporal. It was (then) Lieutenant Hazard, just reporting in to S-2, who'd asked the battalion commander for one last chance with the corporal who was about to get busted back to PFC. The battalion commander had granted Hazard his request, with the caveat that should Corporal Fog stray once more off the hallowed path set by centuries of Marines, it would be Lt. Hazard who would share the blame.

Corporal Fog had enjoyed his first four years as a Marine, but after being involuntarily extended three times, his patience for the Corps had ended. He was bitter and wanted out. But that didn't mean he was stupid. Luckily, the new lieutenant seemed to grasp Fog's predicament. He'd basically told Fog, "You take care of me, and I'll take care of you."

And so they'd become inseparable. Both men were bachelors, and the only thing either of them had was time. Cpl. Fog taught Lt. Hazard what he knew about Marine intelligence, much of which wasn't taught in formal Marine Corps intelligence schools. In return, Lt. Hazard started the frustrating process of dealing with the twisted chain of Marine Corps bureaucracy, with the chief aim of helping Cpl. Fog out of the Corps.

With his extensive field experience and high intellect, Cpl. Fog was the perfect teacher. Lt. Hazard listened and learned. Pretty soon every company commander was coming to Hazard instead of the captain who ran the S-2 shop. Hazard never took the credit, always focused on supporting the companies and platoons. Fog appreciated that and even got swept up in his lieutenant's wake.

One month after their first deployment together (Fog's ninth), Lt. Hazard walked into Cpl. Fog's barracks with a grave look. Fog's stomach dropped. He knew it without being told. He was being extended again.

"Sir, before you say anything, I know how much you've tried—"

Hazard silenced him with an upraised hand. Not just an upraised hand, an upraised hand holding a single sheet of paper. When Fog's eyes looked back up to the lieutenant's face, Hazard's eyes were bright.

"It's official, Marine, the Corps no longer wants a free-loading shitbird like you," Hazard said, trying his best not to smile. "You are to report to S-1 to begin out-processing no later than zero eight hundred tomorrow."

"But how did you—"

Hazard stopped him again.

"I am not finished, Corporal Shitbird. Thanks to the skills I have acquired from watching you, you will find in this folder," he produced a manila folder from behind his back, "a handsomely written recommendation letter, endorsed by myself and the battalion commander."

"Sir, you didn't have to—"

Hazard waved his hand for silence, his face twisted in mock indignation.

"Furthermore, Corporal Shitbird, in said folder you will find the contact information for the man in the Crazy Idiots Agency, which you may know as the CIA, who I am told is looking for shitbirds like you to fill many holes in their ever-leaky bucket."

It was exactly what Fog had wanted. He hadn't known that Hazard was doing it. It was one Marine helping another. A final gesture of friendship from a real leader.

"Thank you, sir," was all he could say.

Hazard's face had softened, and he'd replied, "You've earned it, Fog."

Julian Fog smiled as he remembered that pivotal moment. He'd gone on to get a job with the CIA, and over the next few years, went from admin to analyst, and now to operative. It hadn't been easy, and not always fun, but every step had prepared him for his current position. Luckily for his old boss, Fog's only focus was threats within the Continental U.S.

And the favor Hazard had asked for was as easy as flipping off a switch.

Fog got up from his seat, grabbed the file he'd compiled on Georgy Varushkin, and headed for the door. It would be good to see Hazard again. It would be that much sweeter if it meant cracking into something no other department had yet accomplished: a look into the inner workings of The Pension.

CHAPTER TWENTY-FIVE

Rex picked us up just as the sun was setting over the crowded skyline. Pastor Walker didn't say a word as he scooted into the middle seat, sandwiched between me and one of Rex's guys. The man's gun sat on his lap, and I saw Walker keep glancing at it like it might go off at any minute.

"Been in town long?" Rex asked from the front passenger seat. He'd turned to face me. The damned guy looked just the same except he now wore his former high and tight in a low regulation cut. Cuss like a sailor, but look like a pro. That was Rex.

I wondered what I looked like to him.

"Not long," I answered.

He nodded, but waited ten minutes until we were tucked away in a two room apartment to continue the conversation. The place smelled like grilled cheese and varnish.

Rex's men went about their business as he ushered the pastor and me into the kitchen.

"Want anything to eat?" he asked, already rooting around in the fridge for something. He pulled out a half-eaten sandwich and took a bite.

"We're good," I said, anxious to get moving. The clock in my head kept ticking, and something told me that Anna's time was short. I had to get there soon.

Some kid who looked like he'd just left Mommy and Daddy for college came into the kitchen. He handed me a black canvas bag that was heavier than it looked. I set it down on the Formica counter and unzipped it. Inside were the weapons I'd asked for, all untraceable according to Rex.

There were two AR-15s with extra magazines, enough to fend off a modest attack. He'd also included a pair of Taurus knockoffs, pistols that anyone in non-gun controlled America could pick up for a couple hundred bucks. They were relatively simple weapons, no fancy sights or rail mounted flashlights. If things went bad, I didn't want the authorities to see it for anything other than a break-in gone wrong.

The last weapon was an arm's length machete in an olive drab sheath. Both ends of the sheath had rectangular metal rings with a strap looped through. I adjusted the loops and tied it on with the sheath tight across my back, the strap running down diagonally from my right shoulder. I unsheathed it a couple times to make sure it wouldn't stick. It didn't. Fluid and easy.

"You planning on hacking your way through the jungle?" Rex asked wryly. Pastor Walker looked like he wanted to throw up.

I shrugged and went back to checking the other weapons. Everything looked serviceable.

"You'll probably want these too," Rex said, tossing me a pair of black tactical gloves.

I nodded my thanks and tried them on. Perfect fit. I wasn't planning on leaving any evidence behind, and there was no reason not to be thorough.

"What's the latest from the objective?" I asked, working

the actions on one of the pistols to make sure the gloves didn't get in the way.

"Finish what you're doing and I'll show you," Rex said, tossing the sandwich wrapper in the trash. "Fucking Russians have been in and out all afternoon. You sure picked a helluva time to run into that hornet's nest."

I didn't reply, just followed him from the kitchen.

His team had set up their surveillance equipment in a bedroom, pushing the bed over on its side and sliding it up against the wall. Rex introduced me to his guys, but I was too focused on the screen of the closest laptop to be very conversational. Wherever they'd mounted the camera gave us a perfect view in through the second floor windows. There, as clear as if we were watching from across the street, was Anna. Her head was moving like she was talking, but whoever she was talking to was off to the side.

I heard Pastor Walker's sharp inhale when he realized who was on the screen.

"Is this live? Is she okay?" he stammered, grabbing the sides of the laptop.

"As far as we can tell, she's fine," Rex said, motioning for the guy at the laptop to move to the side.

"But how do you know? Have they hurt her? Is she in danger?" Walker asked, his former bout of courage crumbling.

"They don't know," I said, pulling him back from the computer. "Listen to me. If you don't pull it together, Anna's chances are shot."

That got his attention. Honestly, it wasn't the truth, but the tears in his eyes told me that he needed a come-to-Jesus.

"What do you want me to do?" he asked.

"I need you to help me get in there," I said, pointing at the monitor.

He glanced at the screen and then back at me.

"What do you mean? I can't—"

That's when I slapped him, hard. I couldn't help it. Everyone in the room stopped as Walker's hand pressed against his cheek.

"That's the last time I hear you say you can't do something, you got me?" He nodded, his eyes wide like a wounded animal. "That girl needs our help. Your daughter needs you. Now, I suggest you say a little prayer to that God you're always talking to because in fifteen minutes, you and I are busting in and getting her out."

EVERYTHING WAS SET. Rex's CIA buddy was taking care of the ambiance. Once Pastor Walker and I were in place, the power to the whole block would be shut off. It was a moonless night. Perfect for what I had in mind.

The Varushkin property was a quick five-minute drive from the apartment. When Rex dropped us off a couple blocks away, he gave me one final word of warning, "Remember, I can't get involved directly. But when you're ready to bug out, let me know."

We exchanged steady looks, and then I walked away, Walker on my heels. The plan was simple. It had to be. I would incapacitate the guards at the front door. Walker was my ammo bearer, shouldering the canvas bag that held the extra AR-15 and the surplus ammunition. His only job was to stay close and keep his head down. If I needed more mags, he would provide them.

The streets were clear, so looking inconspicuous was easy. As we moved closer to the objective, I thought about the insanity of the situation. I was about to conduct a solo raid against a fortified position in the middle of Boston. It made me smile.

Rex had mentioned something about Anna's grandfather and how his CIA buddy wanted first dibs on the intel, but I wasn't really listening. My only focus was Anna. After that, her mother. I savored the thought. Anyone who would blackmail her ex-husband, put her own daughter in harm's way, and run a human trafficking organization deserved to be taken down. I wondered if the duchess knew about the guy at the car wash yet.

A half a block away, my earpiece crackled and Rex's voice came through.

"We have multiple vehicles coming from the opposite direction. It looks like they're headed your way."

Even as he said it, I could see the lights coming up ahead. I grabbed Walker's arm and pulled him back, taking cover behind some steps leading up to a townhouse.

"Stay down," I ordered, peering through the railing, the assault rifle cradled and ready.

"They're slowing," I heard Rex say.

I watched the lead vehicle turn, right down the street where we were headed. The three matching dark SUVs followed.

My gut told me to run, to make my move, but I surprised myself by waiting. The seconds slipped by.

"They stopped in front of the house," Rex said. "We've got men coming out, entering the vehicles."

"How many?" I asked.

"Hold on."

The thumping in my chest turned into deep hollow thuds.

"Twelve," Rex said.

"And the girl?" I asked.

"No girl."

What the hell?

"What are they doing now?"

"They're turning around. Wait. Yeah, they're going the way they came."

"What about the guards at the front door?"

"They're gone too," Rex said. "Daniel, I've got a bad feeling..."

I didn't hear the rest of his words. I broke from cover and sprinted toward where the last SUV was that had just rounded the corner. I stuck to the darkness along the edge of the bricked properties. When I hit the left turn, I stopped, looked, and confirmed that the front door was no longer defended. My heart raced faster and I took off without waiting for Anna's father.

When I grabbed the door handle, it was locked. It took me all of twenty seconds to pick the lock. They hadn't set the two deadbolts.

I slithered inside, weapon scanning. No one there. I heard Walker behind me, but ignored him.

Taking the steps to the second floor two at a time, my mind wandered to familiar morbidity. Would I find Anna dead, her blood covering the floor as her blue eyes stared blankly at the ceiling? Had they killed her and run off, or had they snuck her out without Rex's surveillance having noticed? I hope for the second option, already cursing myself for not acting sooner, for not doing something back at the farm, for not staying on that goddamn train and heading to Canada instead.

There was no one on the second floor landing, and all I heard was the buzzing of adrenaline in my ears. I shook my head to clear the sound as I crept closer to the door that would give me my answer. Six more steps and I was there.

I hesitated. Did I really want to see what was inside? Had I done it again? Had my presence led to the death of a child, a girl who could've given the world so much more than I ever could?

I cursed God and the devil in that moment, calling them both motherfuckers for everything they did to screw with our lives. Were we all just pawns in some twisted cosmic game?

Why did everything good in our lives always get taken away and shattered before our eyes? Why couldn't we just be left alone, to live and die as we pleased? *Why, why, WHY?!*

I took a shaky breath, reached for the handle, and opened the door.

CHAPTER TWENTY-SIX

The room was dark. Slivers of color filtered in from the lights on the street. I swept the space with my eyes and my weapon. I stopped and stared. Two ice blue eyes stared back from the corner. *Anna*, my mind whispered.

No, not Anna, but the same eyes. They didn't move, like a ghost. As my vision adjusted I saw that it wasn't a ghost, but a man. He had stark white hair and hollow cheeks. He could've been dead if his gaze hadn't followed me as I continued my scan. I felt no malice from the man, only curiosity. Just like Anna. Where was she?

That was not the case with the second man I found, his own weapon extended and pointed back at me. We locked eyes and I saw that he was just as determined. He had the unwavering look of a dog protecting its master, his own safety secondary.

"You must be Daniel," said the man in the corner, his clear voice cutting across the room. I watched him out of the corner of my eye, weapon and body still focused on the man with the gun. Something else stirred in the corner.

"Daniel?" came a tired voice.

The heat in my chest rippled.

"Anna?" I asked.

"Put the gun down, Vasily. This man is a friend of our Anna's," the man in the corner said.

The guard dog did as ordered, even re-holstering his weapon. I did not reciprocate the gesture. Instead, I swiveled my weapon back to the old ghost in the corner.

"Get up, Anna. We're going," I said.

Her response wasn't what I expected. Instead of running to my side, she stood from the day bed and wrapped her arms around the man who I could now see was sitting in a wheelchair.

"I won't leave him," she said, defiance mingled with worry.

"Anna, your father's just down the hall. We need to leave now," I said, my jaw tight, my gaze unwavering.

She looked hopefully to the door and then back at the man in the wheelchair. He looked at Anna and patted her hand. Then his cool eyes came back to me.

"How did you get in?" he asked.

"It doesn't matter. I need to take Anna, now." My voice was sharp. I didn't have to sit there gabbing with the old man. The hairs on the back of my neck prickled against my collar. It was time to go.

"The guards. Where are the guards?" he asked. There wasn't an ounce of desperation in his voice, just the patient level tone of a general.

"They're gone. They all left. Now, Anna, can we please go?"

My earpiece crackled and I went to turn the volume down, but the look in the old man's eyes stopped me. Recognition.

"What do you know?" I asked, my heart jacking into a higher rhythm.

The old man looked at me for a moment, then back over at Anna.

"You should go," he said to her.

"But I want you to come with us, Poppa."

Poppa? What the hell?

"Daniel," the old man said, turning to me. "You must take Anna and go."

"No! I won't go. You can't make me." She sounded like a child now.

"Anna, listen to me. Go with Daniel. He will see to your safety."

My earpiece crackled again and I heard Rex say something, but his voice was garbled. Anna and the old man were whispering back and forth. I cut in.

"Why the sudden urgency?" I asked him, trying to listen to the radio at the same time.

If he was worried, he didn't show it. It reminded me of the look of old buddies, guys who'd seen war, who'd faced down the enemy's rounds and come out different. Not damaged, just different.

"The reason you must leave, and take Anna with you, is that if I am right, my daughter is about to send men to kill me."

As if in answer to his warning, three things happened almost all at once. First, I heard Rex say, "Five tangos coming in through the front door." Second, I heard Pastor Walker's own warning. A harshly whispered, "Someone's here," from the hallway. Third, whoever was at the front door. I heard a crash, followed by a rush of footsteps.

"Get down," I said to Anna, then ran out the door. The other Russian, Vasily, came right behind, his weapon at the ready.

The bad guys were heading toward the stairs. I took out the first guy with a shot to the head. A lucky shot since I was moving and so was he. The blood spatter made the next man hesitate. Brain chunks to the face will do that. I took that guy out with a quick burst to the chest. He must not have been wearing protection because red blossomed from the front of his white shirt.

Shouts from below. Russian accents. Confusion.

The three guys who were left returned fire as Vasily and I dove for cover. The wood railing and the wall behind me were getting chewed up good. Splinters and dust coated my head as I waited for a shot. The Russian looked to me for direction. I motioned with my fingers that we'd go on the count of three, and that he was to go farther away from the stairs, deeper into the hall. He nodded. Walker was curled up in a ball a few feet away. I motioned for him to stay put. He did not nod back.

By the way the rounds were moving to the side, I knew someone was making their way up the stairs. His companions were shifting fire to accommodate his movement. I counted to three soundlessly, and low-crawled to the steps. Bullets hammered into the top step, throwing more debris into my face. But then I heard firing from behind me. It was the Russian. The firing from below shifted again and I took a chance.

Peeking over the demolished step I saw the guy on the stairs now focused on my new friend. He almost got his weapon around, but the rounds from my pistol caught him under the chin. He staggered back and then over, tumbling down the steps.

There was more shouting from the first floor, and I watched in slow motion as a grenade sailed up and over the railing, heading straight for Vasily. *Shit*. To my complete amazement, the guy actually shot up, caught it in mid-air and rifled it back down to the first level. I heard it hit the floor, and then the explosion rocked the house.

I peered over the lip of the landing, and for a second saw

nothing but dust. When it settled, I saw that one of the guys had caught the brunt of the blast, his legs and torso a meaty mess. The last guy was crawling to the door. He was moaning like a deaf mute, a streak of blood trailing behind his excruciating progress.

I got to him before he touched the door. One eye was shut and oozing red. The other looked up at me, all glazed and dying. We stared at each other as the light faded from his eyes and his head slumped to the floor like his body was deflating.

We'd gotten lucky. If they were expecting a fight, I assumed they would've sent more men. But these guys were dressed in flashy suits like modern day gangsters, all pinstripes and gold chains. They should've come in with tactical gear on and vests full of ammo. Unlucky for them. Maybe Hell would give allowances for spiffy dress.

I checked to make sure they were all dead and then went back upstairs. When I stepped into the room, Pastor Walker was holding his daughter in a crushing embrace, his sobs shaking them both.

"We need to go," I said. I'd radioed Rex on the way up, and he'd promised a ride in two minutes.

Walker looked up but didn't let go of Anna.

"Okay," he choked out, like saying any more would induce another round of sobs.

Before I could ask the old man if he needed any help, Vasily bent down to wheelchair level and hoisted the skinny man out of his seat. He'd been a tall man in his day. Now all he had were lifeless skinny legs that flopped when they moved. The protector cradled the protectee like he'd done it a thousand times. He walked over to me and the old man held out his long-fingered hand.

"I don't know how I can thank you, Daniel."

I took the hand. It was cold and bony, like a skeleton.

"You can tell me who you are," I said, "and then we need to get out of here."

He smiled and said, "My name is Georgy Varushkin."

I nodded. "You're Anna's grandfather."

He nodded back.

"I'm sure we'll have time to get to know one another soon," he said formally. "Now, if you would be so kind as to escort us out, Daniel."

I let go of his hand and headed for the door. There were so many things running through my head, the most important being, who was this guy who'd just sat through an intense fire-fight and now acted like he'd just attended the opera? I shook my head as I hit the stairs. I couldn't wait to find out more about the enigmatic Georgy Varushkin.

CHAPTER TWENTY-SEVEN

The night outside was still, like the world was waiting. It made Natasha want to hold her breath. She resisted the urge, focusing instead on the cars passing by far below, the twinkling of faraway stars and the occasional roar of an airplane overhead. She tried to focus on the calmness of it all, the monotony that was everyday life for millions of ordinary citizens all around. As hard as she tried, she could not find peace.

She'd learned not to look back, not to second guess her decisions. It wasn't healthy. It wasn't conducive to the life swirling around her. Chaos hid in tight corners, waiting for her to relax, let down her guard. Natasha would not. There was no time for second guessing, no time for regret.

And yet she found herself thinking of her father. The first memory she had of him was on a boat. Of course it was on a boat; her father loved the sea. It was in his bones, like he'd been bred from some underwater creature who'd somehow adapted to live on land.

Natasha remembered the crashing of the waves and the

fear that clutched her chest. But her father was there, holding her, reassuring her. That was when she knew that as long as her father was there, she would be safe.

That feeling became a crutch as the years passed. As her father busied himself with business and the requisite travel back to Russia, Natasha was often left with an ever-changing collection of nannies. Normal toddler fussing led to raging temper tantrums. Petty thievery led to blackmail. After the age of eight, no nanny lasted more than two months.

When her father sent her to a boarding school in Colorado, thirteen-year-old Natasha disappeared for three days. She was finally found in the basement of the headmaster's home.

It was never that way when the elder Varushkin was home. As the only female left in the immediate family, Natasha doted on her father, instructed the house staff on the food he liked and even helped cook meals and serve him. She never acted up when he was home.

But he was not always home. For every day he spent in their upper class home, he spent three overseas.

The downward spiral almost derailed the family; it almost cost her father's position within The Pension. His compatriots worried that if he could not handle his own daughter, how was he to handle the immense responsibility of transplanting a population? He'd assured those powerful men of his conviction, and then gave his daughter the only tongue lashing he would ever unleash. After moving her to tears, Georgy Varushkin looked down at his eighteen-year-old daughter and crumpled to his knees, soothing her as he cried too.

After that day, Natasha had been more careful. Instead of hurting her father, she hurt herself. She knew he knew, but he never said a word unless she asked for help. He was old-fashioned that way. He'd rather pretend everything was okay instead of admonishing his family.

But now his old-fashioned ways had collided with the new world, a world she'd helped build. His naivety about the way things really worked had at first confused her. It could be reasoned that prison had softened him. It was understandable. Who wouldn't come out changed?

If Natasha was being honest, she would admit that relinquishing power and control to her father had been a bitter task. She'd known all along that he would return, but it didn't make it any easier to cede her perch.

The Pension needed strong leadership with a forward-thinking vision. If her father had embraced her efforts, had applauded all that she had accomplished, Natasha would have stepped aside gracefully.

That hadn't happened. Initial applause led to blatant accusation. He wanted to dismantle an important cog in her carefully constructed machine. Natasha saw it as a vital ace up her sleeve, a piece that would ensure The Pension's security for years.

No. She would not do it. She would not let go of everything she'd built. And as the hours had passed, she'd gotten to the heart of their disagreement. Put simply, they would never agree. On some level they never really had. Her father was the old man from the sea, ever proper and loyal to a fault. She was part of the new generation, with the energy and enthusiasm to attack every angle, utilize any advantage she could. Hers was the better way.

And that was why she'd ordered her own father's murder. It was why she'd asked Joe to do it now and not later. To drag it out would have been to leave the wound gaping. Better to cauterize the gash and move on. It was a pity that her daughter had to die too, but she felt no connection to the brat anyway. To see the connection between her father and

Anna had only made the decision easier. Be done with it. Move on and forget the past.

But the nagging sense of doubt remained. A small voice whispered in her subconscious, the voice of her own mother maybe? *There was always another way.*

The knocking snapped Natasha from her reverie.

"Come in," she said.

Joe walked into the room. He was wearing a brown silk robe that barely covered his protruding belly.

"I have news," he said, his face tight.

Natasha waited. He looked perturbed, like someone had just shit in his bubble bath.

"My men never returned," he said, searching her for an answer. She did not offer one.

"I've sent more men to see what happened. The first team should have called by now. Is there anything you've forgotten to tell me about your father's companion?"

She rolled her eyes and did her best to appear calm.

"I told you. He had one man with him whom I never saw armed with more than a pistol."

But even as she said it, unease crept into her belly. She'd never heard back from Adam Eplar. Could her ex-husband have gotten the drop on her assassin? That was impossible. The man didn't own a set of balls big enough to take on the former Russian operator.

"If I find out that one man took out my team..."

"Then I'd suggest you recruit men better suited for the job," Natasha snapped.

Joe was sucking in air through his flattened nose. Nostrils expanded and contracted like a bull staring down a matador. Finally, he smiled.

"Maybe you're right. Maybe it is time for some new blood." He closed the gap between them. She could smell the champagne on his breath. He was always drinking champagne. *Veuve Clicquot* because that's what the rappers were always talking about. Joe's hand reached out, touched her hip and then slid around until it held her right buttock. She didn't move. "Tell me," he said. "Is there anyone you can recommend?" He squeezed her rear and it took everything she had not to lash out. She was in his home. It was part of the bargain, a necessary concession until her father's assassination was complete and they could formalize their merger.

"I'm sure I can think of a few names," she said.

He smiled and removed his hand, already making his way to the door.

"I was just getting ready to take a bath. Feel free to join me if you'd like," he said over his shoulder.

"I'll think about it," she replied, returning his grin with a playful wink.

Once he had left, Natasha grabbed her phone and thought about who she should call first. If their most recent conversation was any indication of where things were going, Natasha had to plan her departure as quickly as possible. She still had a closet full of surprises that would keep Joe from nipping at her heels. Maybe she'd been too hasty in calling her rival. But as soon as she thought it, the indecision melted away.

Asking her people to kill someone like her ex-husband was one thing. Asking them to kill her father, the great Georgy Varushkin, whom they all looked up to like a modern day Godfather, would be impossible. That would have eroded her support base and likely her chance at heading The Pension. She wouldn't risk that, and once again, the Russian mobster down the hall was her necessary evil.

Natasha resisted the urge to make a phone call. She didn't know if Joe had the room bugged. It would be slower to send a secure message through one of her many bogus Facebook accounts, but at least Joe couldn't track it. It took less than a minute to write the brief message and store it in the only group frequented by that profile.

Her work now done, Natasha returned to the spot by the window, once again trying to be hypnotized by the blinks and swirls of the night.

CHAPTER TWENTY-EIGHT

R ex was waiting when we pulled up to the curb. It had
started to rain, and he held an oversized golf umbrella
as we piled out of the van. The umbrella got passed to Pastor
Walker, who held it over himself and Anna. She gave me a
weak smile as she walked by, like she wasn't sure how to act
around me.

I'd seen that look before. Everything was roses and rainbows until they saw you kill someone, or in this case, multiple
someones. I couldn't tell if that's what she was thinking, or if
she was just exhausted. She hadn't said a word on the ride
over. Her silence was a concern. She'd been my only reason
for going in. I shouldn't have cared about what some fifteen-
year-old girl thought about me, especially one I barely knew,
but I did.

I nodded to Mr. Varushkin as his body servant hoisted
him out of the car. If he cared about the fat raindrops soaking
his hair, he didn't show it. In fact, just before they got to the
back door, I saw Varushkin motion for his man to stop.
When he did, Varushkin looked up at the sky and closed his

eyes. The rain pelted his face, but I swear I saw a little smile there. After a moment, he touched Vasily's arm, and they entered the apartment complex.

"We need to talk," Rex said, his tone unreadable. I could only imagine what he was thinking. I'd just killed a bunch of thugs in public. There had to be a thousand laws screaming in Rex's head, telling him to turn me in instead of helping me.

"Can we go inside?" I said, wiping a sheet of water from my forehead.

He nodded and we stepped out of the downpour.

THERE WERE MORE men in the apartment this time. By the way they mingled with Rex's guys, I knew they weren't his.

"Who are they?" I asked.

"New friends," he answered, already moving past me. "Come on. I've got someone I want you to meet."

What I really wanted was a hot shower and a bed. I didn't like taking orders, and I had to remind myself that Rex was doing me the big favor, not the other way around. It was best to go along with whatever he had in mind now. Better to stay in his good graces if my next play was going to succeed.

I entered the spare bedroom and locked eyes with the guy sitting in the corner. He had a laptop perched on one of those TV trays, the kind with legs that everyone in the Eighties used to use when someone was sick. He was somewhere between skinny and wiry. I'd call it scrappy. He looked at me with an amused grin. He did not bother getting up to shake my hand when Rex introduced him.

"Daniel Briggs, this is Julian Fog, another intel weenie who was lucky enough to start his life stepping on yellow footprints on Parris Island."

Fog nodded. I returned the gesture.

"Have fun?" Fog asked after appraising me for another long moment.

"Sorry?" I answered, trying to figure out whether he was a run-of-the-mill smart ass or born-and-bred wise ass.

"I said, did you have fun? With the Russians?"

He wasn't being sarcastic. He really wanted to know.

"It had to be done," I answered truthfully.

Fog nodded thoughtfully, like I'd passed his test.

"Is the girl okay?"

"She is."

He nodded again.

"And the grandfather?" This question he directed at Rex.

"The old man is in the other apartment," Rex said, as much to me as to his buddy.

"You think I could have a word with him?"

Rex looked to me. I shrugged. "You'll have to ask him."

"What do you know about him?" Fog asked, stretching his legs like he'd been sitting for hours.

"I just met him."

"He didn't say anything?"

My eyes went from Fog, to Rex, and back to Fog.

"Look, guys, I'm fucking tired. Why don't you tell me who you're with," I pointed at Fog, "and what you want to know, and then let me get some sleep?"

Rex finally smiled and gave Fog one of those "I told you so" looks.

Fog chuckled.

"Sorry." This time he got up from his seat and walked over. "Julian Fog at your service. At one time I was a paper pusher under then Lieutenant Hazard's strict watch. You don't recognize me?"

I studied his face for a minute. He had one of those plain haircuts and average faces that blends into any Marine formation. I'd seen thousands of the same face during my time in the Corps.

"Should I?"

Fog grinned and shook his head.

"We served together, but there's no reason you should remember me. I was in S-2 and you were busy making a name for yourself."

He didn't say it like a lot of others did, like he was awed by my accomplishments. It was just a statement of fact, two Marines discussing extraordinary events the same way they discussed the weather.

"You didn't say who you work for," I said, warming to Julian Fog. If Rex knew him and trusted him, maybe I should do the same.

"To most people I'm an independent contractor, a security specialist who dabbles in high-end stereo equipment and residential alarm systems. Officially, I am an employee of the Central Intelligence Agency."

I grunted. Funny how one phone call to a friend turns into the thunder of cavalry.

"And you're here because...?"

"Our buddy Rex here was having a hard time finding information on your mysterious Russian. It turns out that Georgy Varushkin, former Soviet Navy Captain turned private businessman, is high on the Persons of Interest list at Langley."

"And you have access to this list?" I asked.

Rex answered for him.

"What Julian has failed to mention is that, like you, he has a certain set of talents that makes him a valuable asset for his employer. Not only is he a top analyst, he is also one of their best domestic operatives. I'd like to think I had a little bit to do with that, but I didn't."

"The hell you didn't," Fog interrupted.

Rex ignored him.

"Julian got creative and got the information that even my boss at the Bureau couldn't get. This Varushkin guy could be a goldmine of intel for the good guys. The question is whether he'll cooperate or not."

"He will," I said without thinking.

"You sure?" Fog asked.

"Yeah."

"Why don't you go see if he'll talk to us now?" Rex said. "No time like the present to get started."

I nodded and went for the door. Rex and the spook could get whatever they wanted from the old man. The only things I wanted to know from him were a) how to find his daughter, and b) how to get my hands around her pretty little neck.

———

GEORGY VARUSHKIN WAS JUST GETTING SETTLED when Daniel came in through the door. Anna's friend and savior was a fascinating confluence of traits to Georgy's practiced eye. There was real pain there, as well as compassion and love, as evidenced by his attachment to Anna. And then there was his physical body, obviously trained and tested at the highest levels. He would undoubtedly pounce on the nearest threat with little thought to his own life. Georgy found himself wanting to know more, wanting to look inside Daniel's mind and tinker with its parts.

The young man nodded to the two guards, and approached the leather recliner where Vasily had propped his weary bones.

"Mr. Varushkin, I was wondering if we could speak to you," Daniel said.

Georgy was tired, exhausted really, but he'd learned to push past that. Prison had shown him that even physical limits could be stretched beyond what the brightest minds would think possible.

Anna and her father were in one of the bedrooms. He'd instructed them to get what sleep they could. He had the time to talk.

"Here?"

"In the next apartment, if that's okay," Daniel answered. His blond savior looked tired as well, but there was a fire there, like glowing coals just waiting to flare to life.

Georgy nodded to Vasily, who picked him up without question, the act now beyond routine.

They followed Daniel next door. Georgy took it all in, the men hunched over computers or discussing something over large mugs of coffee. Some of them looked up as he passed. Surely he must look quite the sight.

The next room they entered was occupied by two men. One he recognized from their arrival, and the other stared at him with obvious curiosity. The thinner man offered him a chair. Vasily sat him down and took up his customary position next to his patron.

"Mr. Varushkin, my name is Julian Fog," the thin man said. "I was hoping you could spare us a few minutes to chat."

Georgy smiled. "Of course. Anything for what you've already done for my family."

"Thank you, sir," said Fog, pulling up a chair to sit across from him.

"May I asked who you work for, Mr. Fog?"

"Please, call me Julian, Mr. Varushkin."

"Then you must call me Georgy."

The two men smiled at one another. Georgy liked this Julian Fog immediately. Despite his small stature, the man exuded confidence and professionalism, like an experienced non-commissioned officer.

"I work for the Central Intelligence Agency," Julian said.

Georgy's heart fluttered, causing his breath to catch. Could it be? Could that blond savior standing in the corner have brought them years ahead of their projections? For a moment, he couldn't find the words to respond.

Julian looked on with concern and asked, "Are you well, Georgy?" It took a good ten seconds for the Russian to realize the question had been asked in Russian.

Now there were tears flooding his eyes, the first dropping to his lap like a lazy bomblet. Georgy shook his head, trying to regain his composure.

"I am sorry," he said. "It is only...I have been in prison, you see. For five years they tortured me, threatened my family, took me to the edge of my life." The tears were flowing freely now, a luxury he'd never once shown during his imprisonment. Like a broken dam, the emotions flowed, the relief cloaking him, the memories of the last five years suddenly pushed away in a flood of elation.

No one said a word as he choked back his words, unable to pinpoint the exact place to start. He felt a hand on his shoulder and looked up to see Vasily, his ever-loyal Vasily, the unwavering steward and friend. Vasily nodded, understanding completely what his master was thinking.

"Tell them," Vasily said, his stoic face now flushed with emotion. He felt it too.

Georgy nodded and turned back to the others. There was a new energy in his chest, like a wellspring of life force urging him to tell his tale. The next time he opened his mouth, the words were crystal clear, like in the old days.

"It all started without my knowledge. I was a very young man, a boy really, when I was chosen. I was trained and mentored by a group of men who saw what would become of the Soviet Union. They had the foresight to see what our failed economic system would result in, what the military race against your country would lead to. They saw the collapse before it happened. I was one of the lucky few to be privy to this secret, to be allowed to prepare for what would eventually happen. So as I climbed the ranks of the Soviet Navy, we strengthened our secret bonds and carefully expanded our reach. By the time the Soviet Union came crashing down, we were ready.

"With our military contacts, we secured surplus material and land that the government could no longer support. The money we'd accrued over the previous decades grew from millions to billions. Not overnight, mind you, but as the Russian economy opened to the world, we broadened our own network, capitalizing on our purchases and leveraging them for more overseas.

"Slowly, we shifted our reserves to international banking institutions. From Japan to the Bahamas we stashed our hard-earned savings. As more and more of the new Russian government came under the old system of bribes and cronyism, we sped up our plans. I was tasked with making a move to the United States. It would be our first foothold in the outside world. We saw the United States as the safest bet, the country most likely to weather future storms. It was the right choice.

"For years I saw to the re-shuffling of money and assets. With our money we bought businesses, real estate, stocks, anything a normal successful American businessman would invest in. It was deemed necessary, in the beginning, to take over a small Russian racket that specialized in smuggling Russian goods into America. We took over their operation after a minor scuffle, and successfully tripled our imports. Unfortunately, some of the old business survives today, despite my orders to the contrary."

Georgy paused as his last conversation with Natasha replayed in his mind. He winced at the memory.

"It was not my intention for that part of our organization

to continue, but it seems that during my internment, certain other individuals saw our situation differently. And before you ask, yes, I am speaking of my own daughter, Natasha. It saddens me to say this. I have tried to be a good father, to raise her without a mother, but I have failed. My sweet Natasha is no more."

He paused again, wiping his eyes on his sleeve.

"I tell you that I love my country, gentlemen. For all its flaws, for all the men who have tried to turn it into their own evil likeness, underneath there will always be Mother Russia. Tyrants come and go. Time does its best to outlast us, but the heart of a Russian is always faithful, always strong. I will always be Russian. It is my dream, it is the dream of the men and women who comprise this organization that we named The Pension, to return to Russia one day and reclaim and rebuild what has been broken.

"It was our plan to reach out to the American government one day, once we'd established our community here on your soil. We would be prepared to share our combined knowledge, to utilize our contacts inside Russia to provide you with the intelligence and data we would need to facilitate a peaceful coup. We had to be careful. Before, we were not careful enough. That was how I was kidnapped and thrown in jail. There were few we could trust. Fewer now."

Georgy thought of his friends whom he'd only recently discovered were now dead. He tried not to think about how his own words, words torn from his soul by his captors, had been used to find and snuff those old friends from being.

"I will never again see my beloved Russia, gentlemen. I know that. But because God sent your friend Daniel to my Anna, maybe we can help one another. I do not believe in coincidences. I believe in doing what is right for my people, for our people. So tell me, Julian, would it be possible for you to keep my secret, to help me do what I have only dreamed?"

Silence in the room. Georgy half-expected someone to laugh, or maybe for a team of black clad men to rush the room and drag him off to a secret detention facility. Neither happened.

Instead, Julian Fog leaned forward and held out his hand, "I think you've landed in the right place, Georgy."

CHAPTER TWENTY-NINE

H er eyes darted. Her hands trembled. Her breath came in labored gasps.

Anna looked up at the Pepto-Bismol colored sky, a screeching calling to her as she scanned. She'd been running. For how long? Anna had no idea. Sluggish, like her feet were pressed into six inches of sticky mud, she trudged on, willing her legs to move faster. They would not heed her call.

She was so focused on the screeches from overhead that she barely noticed as the skyline turned violet and then ever-green. Her heart pounded as she searched the sky and the hard packed ground below. What was she looking for? What was following her? Where was she going?

A black shadow passed overhead. Anna ducked, but the flying thing was too high to touch her. It did let out an ear-splitting screech as it soared by. A warning maybe?

Her instincts told Anna to protect herself. Other than her bare hands there was nothing in sight that she could use. Even when she bent down to touch a clump of lazy grass, the feel was foreign and incorporeal, like a ghost.

A dream, she muttered, her own voice sounding muffled and strange.

She'd always heard that it was possible to control dreams, and she'd even done a fair amount of research into doing just that. But no matter how hard she tried, the control was always just out of reach.

Once she understood that nothing was real, even though her body was telling her differently, she stopped moving. The shadow returned. Anna waited. The bird thing came closer, calling angrily from fifty, then twenty feet in the air. Anna stood her ground, squinting against the glare of the fake sun, trying to get a glimpse of the creature.

A cloud must have appeared overhead, because a larger shadow enveloped the flying beast, and Anna bit her lip. Whatever the thing was, it had an enormous wingspan. When it was ten feet away, the animal reared back, its wings spread wide, buffeting Anna with a gust of dream wind.

The thing's face was obscured like things tend to be in dreams, but Anna saw the rest of the animal in dark clarity. Wings covered in shimmering obsidian feathers. A chest of blazing red like a suit of armor.

"Anna," the thing said.

Anna's head shot up, willing the haze surrounding the beast's face to melt away.

"Who are you?" Anna asked, brave enough to take step closer.

"You know who I am," the animal said, its voice garbled like it was using one of those voice modulators. It didn't sound male or female.

"I don't know who you are," Anna replied, more confused than scared.

The winged creature chuckled and said, "Ah, but you know who this is."

Anna almost asked what the thing was talking about, but

noticed the twitching of the beast's muscular leg, like it was shifting its weight from one side to the other.

She looked to the ground and clamped a hand over her mouth.

There, clasped in one of the massive red talons of the beast, was the bloody body of her father. His face was upturned and staring into nothingness. He was dead. Anna bit back her scream, reminded her brain that it was all just a dream. *Just a dream.*

Then she heard another sound, like scraping claws. Anna looked to her right and saw a figure on the ground, maybe twenty feet away. The blue eyes she recognized immediately. It was her grandfather. He was crawling toward her, his face contorted in pain, his cheeks covered with dirt. He was saying something she couldn't quite hear. She moved closer. Her grandfather stopped moving. That's when she noticed his legs, or where his legs were supposed to be. There was nothing below his waist, nothing except some bubbling ooze that trailed back the way he'd come.

He looked up at her with pitiful eyes, and then his head slumped to the ground.

What did it all mean?

Anna turned back to the beast. It still held her father's body, perched on it actually. As Anna's eyes drifted back up the body, the thing's shape changed. It became more feminine, with slight curves that resembled a woman's body under a layer of feathers.

When her gaze reached the top, where an oversized beak should have been, Anna's eyes bulged at the beast's visage. It was her mother: beautiful, elegant Natasha.

"Come with me, Anna. It's time to go home," her mother-beast said in a soothing purr.

Anna backpedaled. She needed to get away. She needed to wake up. But no matter how hard she tried, the dream kept playing. On and on it went, her mother still calling to her, the ooze from her grandfather spreading until it covered Anna's feet and slowed her progress further. The panic filled her chest and threatened to collapse her knees to the ground.

One thought came to mind as the death scene continued, Anna's heart racing to find a way out.

Where is Daniel?

———

THREE HOURS of sleep was all I was going to get. Rex and Fog's boys were all working when I got up just after four in the morning. There were two coffee pots simmering in the kitchen, and I helped myself to a mug of it, black.

No one looked up. No one engaged me. Had Rex spread the word that I was to be left alone? It wouldn't have surprised me. He'd always had a way of clearing my path and letting me stay on task.

I watched the others working as I sipped at the coffee. The cobwebs were long gone when the apartment door opened and Anna stepped inside with a short stocky guy who'd been guarding the extra apartment. The guard pointed at me and Anna nodded.

Her eyes were swollen yet clear. I gestured to the coffee when she'd made her way across the room.

"Yes, please," she said, grabbing a mug from the stack and watching as I poured from the pot.

"Want anything in it?"

She shook her head and sipped from the steaming cup.

We stood there for a minute, not saying anything, just two people sharing a quiet coffee before sunrise.

"Where's your dad?" I asked, growing uncomfortable with her silence.

"He was sleeping when I left."

I nodded. Anna sipped her coffee.

"Are you okay?" Anna asked.

"Shouldn't I be the one asking you that question?" This girl was full of surprises.

"I'm fine," she said.

I didn't press. We stood in silence for another couple minutes.

"What are you going to do now?" Anna asked.

My insides froze, but I took a sip of coffee anyway.

"I don't think you want to know," I answered.

"You're going after my mom, aren't you?"

I didn't want to talk about that with Anna. My plans were my plans. A little girl shouldn't have to hear about it. I didn't answer. She got the point.

"What makes people bad?" she asked.

Where is she going with this?

"In what sense?"

"You know, in your opinion, what makes someone go from good to bad?"

Where did she come up with this stuff?

I'd seen plenty of bad things in my life. Hell, I'd killed plenty of bad people. But I'd never thought about what led them to my crosshairs.

"I don't know. Circumstances. Family. Mental health?" I said.

"Did you feel bad after killing those men?"

"No," I answered without hesitation.

"Are you sure?"

"Yeah, I'm sure."

"So when you have bad dreams, it's not about the people you've killed?"

I hesitated answering. I'd never told anyone about what happened in my sleep.

I stared at Anna and tried to understand what made some

kids more resilient than others. Was it bred or was it given by some power we couldn't see? Why was Anna, only hours after almost getting killed, able to talk about my deep dark secrets in the nonplussed manner of a supervising physician? The kid had a strength that I admired, that I found myself wishing for. What gave an innocent like Anna the key to unlocking my inner sanctum, a place that I'd padlocked, boarded and cemented shut? My own private torture chamber.

Whatever it was, Anna's words cracked the code. Words spilled out of my mouth. All I could do was listen along with her.

"No, it's never about the people I've killed," my voice said.

"Then what is it? What are your nightmares about?"

I wanted to walk out the door and keep walking. My inner beast begged me to. It growled in frustration and moaned when my mouth opened again.

"I dream about the people I couldn't save, the friends I couldn't protect. I see their faces and know I could have done more."

I felt numb. The voices in my head went mute. I waited for her reply.

She was staring at me again. I couldn't read her expression. It was like my senses had dulled, leaving me plain and average. I felt naked.

Anna grinned. My eyes narrowed. Her grin turned into a smile. My eyes softened.

"Thank you for telling me," she said, her eyes sparkling.

I didn't get it. She was supposed to be repulsed. Even the therapist the Corps made me see looked at me like I should be locked up. Why was this fifteen-year-old girl looking at me like I was something special?

"You're not disgusted," I said.

She shook her head, the beaming smile still there. It made me uncomfortable.

"And what would you say if I told you that I'm going to find your mother and kill her?"

That wiped the smile from her face. I wanted to give her all the details, everything that was inside of my head. Maybe then she would see the monster standing in front of her. She thought I was some kind of hero, someone to look up to, a friend that would always be there.

I'd proved those assumptions wrong. How many had I let down? How many friends had depended on me only to meet the reaper?

Anna set her coffee on the counter and glanced at the door.

"Maybe I should go," she said.

"I think that's best."

She nodded and rejoined the guard who'd escorted her over. When the door was closed again, I let out a silent exhale. I needed to get things wrapped soon and get back on the road. It felt like someone was laying booby traps all around me, begging me to step forward. I was trapped and claustrophobic. Maybe a walk would help clear my head.

I didn't say a word to anyone as I left. No one stopped me. Maybe I could keep walking. My backpack was in the apartment, but other than some old clothes, there wasn't anything I needed. Rex and his CIA buddy could take care of the Varushkins. They could probably do it without getting any of their men killed.

I was halfway to the stairwell when Anna's voice called from behind.

"Daniel."

I turned, reluctant to revisit our conversation. No doubt she wanted to tell me how awesome I really was, how God made me into this amazing tool that I would one day understand. She still had the innocence of youth, and after my snap about her mother, I was hesitant to snatch more of that innocence from her.

"What's up?" I asked.

When she came closer her features were twisted in confusion, or was it fright? Not one but two guards were right behind her.

Oh crap. Now what?

"Dad's gone," she said, her voice thick with panic.

"What? How did he—?"

One of the guards answered for her, "He climbed out the window. Tied the sheets together to lower himself down."

"And he left this note," Anna said, handing me a folded sheet of loose leaf paper.

It was short. I recognized the pastor's chicken scratch.

*Anna, I have to go. I'm going to make things right. Tell Daniel that
I'm sorry, that he was right.
I love you so much.
- Dad*

FUCK. Now what was I supposed to do?

CHAPTER THIRTY

Her assassin was dead. Her father had disappeared. Despite the pile of unwanted news, all was far from lost.

Natasha turned over in the king size bed and looked at the neon green numbers on the clock for perhaps the fiftieth time. It was almost six in the morning and she'd only slept in spurts. A sleeping pill would've been the normal antidote, but sleeping under the volatile Joe's roof kept her on edge. She'd made all the arrangements she could, and still her brain churned through every detail.

She closed her eyes again and focused on breathing. One long breath in. One long breath out. Natasha never made it to the next breath.

The light knocking on the door jolted her back to reality, although her body remained immobile.

"Yes?" she called out, not turning on the light as she gripped the pistol under her pillow.

"It's Joe. I have a surprise."

Natasha wanted to tell the fool to go away. It wasn't even light out and already her host was making passes. Her body shuddered at the thought of that man touching her again.

"Can it wait?" she asked, smoothing her hair and blinking rapidly to clear her vision.

"I think you will enjoy what I have to show you."

Natasha slid out of bed and grabbed the fluffy white robe she'd been provided. The cut was a a a bit short, no doubt an intentional choice by her host. Her sculpted legs were impossible to miss in the borrowed attire. She was past caring. Besides, the pockets were large enough to conceal her pistol.

When she opened the door, Joe's grinning face was waiting. He was fully dressed and held a crystal glass half full of orange juice.

"I am sorry to have woken you," he said.

"I was awake."

"Good. Now, would you like to see your surprise?"

Natasha nodded. Joe led her down the hall and into the main living space. There was a group of Joe's men milling near the couches. They stopped talking when their boss entered.

What now? Natasha wondered.

Joe gestured impatiently for his men to move away. When they did, Natasha got her first glimpse of Joe's surprise.

The man's nose was bleeding and his shirt was torn. He'd been beaten, but not badly. He looked up when Natasha approached, a medley of emotions on the man's face.

"Well hello, Eddie," she said to her ex-husband.

"Natasha," Pastor Walker answered almost under his breath.

Natasha turned back to Joe.

"Where did you find him?"

Joe laughed and pointed at the pastor.

"The idiot showed up at your house."

Natasha turned back to her ex.

"Now that wasn't very smart, Eddie."

His eyes narrowed, but he held his tongue.

"What do you want me to do with him?" Joe asked.

Natasha thought about it for a moment. No doubt Joe wanted to have some fun with her old fling. He was a bully. She'd heard the stories of his notorious torture rooms.

"Take him to the meeting place," she said. "Get him cleaned up."

Joe looked disappointed.

"And, Joe," she continued, "Keep your hands to yourself."

————

JULIAN FOG'S stock kept rising. When I'd stormed back into our hasty HQ after Pastor Walker's disappearance, Fog had calmly explained that he'd planted a tracking beacon in the pastor's shoe. "We can't use it continuously, but we can ping it when needed."

Instead of sending out a team to snatch the pastor, Fog had recommended we wait.

"My gut says he could lead us right to Mr. Varushkin's daughter."

So we'd waited and we'd watched.

The pastor's first stop was the scene of our most recent encounter with the Russian goons. While that surprised us at first, once we discussed it, the plan made sense. How else would he find his ex-wife?

An hour after pinging at the brownstone, Fog's beacon showed Walker at a location somewhere across the water in East Boston, closer to the airport. By then we were mobile again. Rex was in charge of finding us a new hideout because of the very real chance that Pastor Walker would crack under interrogation. Until then we were scattered in Fog's rented vans.

Fog went over the various assets he had at his disposal as we rumbled over more potholes.

"I've got access to all the major agencies here in Boston. If we need to disguise a team as bus drivers, we can do it. If we need to go in as members of the Port Authority, no problem."

My plan was to stay out of the way. I didn't want to say it when Anna was around, but her dad wasn't my responsibility. I had one target in mind, and if slow-tracking Anna's dad could get me there, I would wait.

By the time we'd made our way through morning traffic, Walker had moved again. The only problem with Fog's tracking device was that it wasn't pinpoint accurate unless you were right on top of it. That didn't matter now. The first ping showed Walker somewhere on the water in Boston Harbor. My mind immediately imagined the worst. Maybe they were taking him out to sea. A bullet in the head and an ocean burial didn't take long. I glanced at Fog and saw he was thinking the same thing. It was a good thing Anna was in another van with her grandfather. She didn't need to see this.

After waiting another ten minutes, Fog pinged the device again. I half expected no return signal on the computer screen. I was wrong.

"Looks like he's on Georges Island," Fog said, zooming in from his aerial view. As the image cleared, I saw that the island was small and vaguely round. There was a structure there, and as the picture reached its max focus, I stared at the screen and counted the five sides, a pentagonal shape, like a star. Walls and exaggerated corners.

"Is that what I think it is?" I asked.

"Fort Warren," Fog replied, pulling up a Wikipedia page on the other half of the screen. He started reading aloud. "Completed during the Civil War. Used as a prison during that war and later as coastal defense. Decommissioned in 1947, it's now a tourist site."

According to the Wikipedia write-up, the island was twenty-eight acres big and the fort was open to the public starting in May and closed sometime around Columbus Day. That gave me an idea.

"Can I borrow your phone?" I asked.

Fog handed over his cell. There was no link to a Fort Warren website, but there was one for Boston Harbor Islands. I dialed the number for customer service. A cheery female voice came on after two rings.

"Boston Harbor Islands," she said.

"Yes, I'm in town for the day, and my kids really want to see one of your island forts. My son loves cannons. He looked it up online and said there's one called Fort Walton?"

I heard her chuckle.

"Did he mean Fort *Warren?*" she asked.

"Yeah, that's it."

"The easiest way is to take the ferry from..."

Her voice trailed off. I heard a keyboard clicking on the other end.

"I'm sorry, sir, did you say you wanted to go today?"

"Yeah, we fly out early tomorrow morning."

"Hmmm. I'm sorry to tell you this, and it is odd for this time of year, but it seems that a private party booked the island for a corporate event."

"Wow. Can they do that?"

"If they pay enough money, yessir, they can," she answered, her tone relaying how she felt about public spaces being hoarded by people with money.

"And there's no way around that?"

"No, sir. There's a note in my system that says they will be setting up beginning this morning."

"And they're using it all day?" I asked, giving her my best frustrated dad tone.

"I'm afraid so. Their security team and catering company

will be there all day and my computer says the party is tonight."

"Maybe I should crash it," I said with a laugh.

"Only if you take me with you," she replied.

I exhaled in mock frustration and said. "Okay, well at least I tried. Thanks for your help."

"Not a problem, sir. We'd love to host you again soon."

I ended the call and handed the phone back to Fog.

"Good news?" he asked.

"As good as it's gonna get, I think. Looks like Natasha Varushkin is throwing a little party. Any way you can get me on that island?"

Fog grinned like I'd just given him the keys to a Ferrari.

"For you? Hell yeah."

CHAPTER THIRTY-ONE

Natasha's people brought the civilian security uniforms over to the island in the early afternoon. Her guests had insisted on independent contractors being on site for the night's festivities. Natasha went along with the demand. The fact that she'd had Joe pay the security company owner a visit didn't need to be public knowledge. It was all part of the show.

Joe's men would assume the security role, protecting Georges Island from prying eyes and unwelcome guests. As she knew he would, Joe demanded to go along. He said he wanted to see Natasha's friends with his own eyes. What he really wanted was to keep tabs on her.

"Fine," Natasha said. "As long as you wear a uniform and leave me to my business, you are welcome to come."

His grin had disappeared when he tried to button the offered uniform and found that his paunch wouldn't allow it. Joe opted for another size and went into his bedroom to finish getting ready. That made Natasha grin.

When everyone was dressed and assembled in the living room, Natasha addressed Joe and his men.

"Our guests have been instructed to arrive by boat just after sunset. Your job is to patrol the island and stay out of sight. Is that understood?"

The men, now clothed in matching blue uniforms and ball caps bearing the logo of Patriot Security Group, all nodded.

"If you have any concerns, they will be relayed to me," Joe said, unable to let Natasha have the last word. "I'm sure Ms. Varushkin will have her hands full."

He winked at Natasha like he was doing her some kind of favor. Natasha smiled back with as much sugar as she could stomach. A few more hours and she'd be rid of the pervert.

———

THE QUICKEST WAY TO get me onto the island was going to be by air. After a clipped phone call, Fog announced there would be a small prop aircraft waiting at a private strip just outside the city.

"It's a four seater, so you can either go alone or take one of my guys," Fog said. The operators were all gathered around the kitchen table in the newly rented safe house.

The plan was to jump in. I didn't have a lot of parachuting experience, but Fog told me that the gear he'd commandeered made it easy to navigate to a precise coordinate. "Keep the compass pointed in the right direction and the gear does the rest," he'd said. Technology rarely worked as well as promised, but I decided to trust Fog in this case. He seemed to have a lot of experience with the nav gear.

"I'm good going in alone." Like my days in the Corps, I'd be in first, the point man getting eyes on the objective. We didn't have access to real-time satellite images or drone video, so my view would relay the disposition of enemy forces on the ground. Fog's boys would come in by water based on my assessment.

"I'll go with him," Rex said, clapping me on the back. "Just like the old days."

My days as a team player were long gone. I resisted the urge to tell him to stay behind, but the look on Rex's face told me it wouldn't do any good. I nodded and turned back to the map.

"I'll drop in on the south end of the island," I said, pointing to the most open terrain there was other than the parade ground in the middle of the fort. Going in from another angle would be a pain. If I did, there were the high fort walls to contend with. There's a reason they call them forts. They're made to keep people out. Coming from the south, at least I'd have the option of using the front door. Who knew. I could get lucky.

"We'll take the northern approach," Fog said. "Shouldn't take much to get over those walls." Funny that Fog was okay with scaling the battlements.

It was a simple plan. The best plans usually were. At least this way if I was found, the others could just swim back to the boat. No sense endangering everyone just because I wanted to get Natasha. If I could find Pastor Walker, so be it, but in my mind he'd made the decision on his own to step into the line of fire.

Even as I thought it, something deep inside told me that I would do anything to save Anna's father. I wouldn't do it for him. I'd do it for her.

———

ANNA TRIED TO ACT CALM. It was what she'd trained herself to do. Whenever her dad freaked out about their lack of food or his inability to provide more for her, she'd always answered with a sincere smile that said everything would be okay.

This time was different. As she listened to her grandfather

talk about his travels, the crash of thirty foot waves and the arduous life of a Soviet sailor, Anna was only half listening. He was trying to distract her and it wasn't working.

Anna thought of her mother, the image from the dream still vivid in her fifteen-year-old mind. Then she would imagine her father, either running for his life or lying lifeless in the clutches of her mother-monster. She shivered as the picture faded from view.

"Are you thinking of them?" her grandfather asked.

She hadn't noticed that he'd stopped his storytelling.

"I can't help it, Poppa."

He nodded and motioned for her to sit next to him. She did.

"What are you most afraid of?" he asked.

"I don't know."

He nodded again.

"Do you know what I am afraid of?"

Anna shook her head, relieved she wasn't the only one.

"I worry for you," he said. "I worry about how this ordeal might change you. The Anna I first met was so full of hope, so full of happiness and life. I would give anything to see that Anna again."

Anna tried to smile. As the corners of her mouth moved, the tears gathered in the eyes.

"I don't know what happens next, Poppa. Tell me what happens next."

She leaned into him and he wrapped her in his arms.

"I wish I knew, Anna. I wish I knew. There is one thing that I will tell you, one thing that kept me going when every day seemed worse than the last."

Anna looked up at her grandfather through tear-clouded eyes.

"Do you know the secret? Do you know how I survived five years of imprisonment?"

Anna shook her head. She wanted the answer. The world seemed to be crumbling all around, but if anyone knew the answer it had to be her grandfather.

His broad smile spread to his eyes and he said, "Hope. It was always hope. As long as you remember to hope, anything is possible."

Anna sniffled and swallowed a whimper. It would take every drop of strength she had to do what her grandfather said. Before, she might have prayed. Now, the will to pray was gone. Hope was slipping away like liquid through her fingers. If she lost everything, how could she ever hope again?

CHAPTER THIRTY-TWO

W e took off an hour before sunset. The pilot, a tight-lipped guy sporting aviator sunglasses and a mane of wild gray hair, suggested we do a couple high passes to get a lay of the land.

"If you're jumping in, better to see what you're jumping into," he said matter-of-factly. It was the last thing he said until we passed over the island. "That's it down there," he said unnecessarily. The star shaped fort at the mouth of the harbor was hard to miss.

We made a long turn out to sea and then swung back in to shore. The next pass was lower, and when I looked down at the fort through high power binoculars, I saw a white tent in the middle of the fort's green parade ground.

There were people bustling around, but I couldn't make out anything except for the color of their clothing. The next thing I saw were the two man teams roaming around the perimeter of the island. They were wearing dark uniforms and kept even spacing as they moved. I counted at least five teams of two. Those were the ones who were visible. There could be more inside the fort or inside the gift and snack shop buildings.

By the time the island faded from view, the sun was sinking in front of us, the last rays of magenta saying goodbye over the horizon. A couple more minutes, and the pilot turned north. I felt the airplane gaining altitude and nudged Rex to check my gear one last time. We were cramped in the back with our chutes and weapons, and the jump out would be tricky, but at least we'd be going in under the cover of night. I had the general layout of the island in my head, and a map printout in my pocket, but that wouldn't help us a bit if one of those roving patrols saw us dropping in. We'd be easy targets.

"You're good," Rex said. He grinned like in the old days. "Into harm's way we go once again."

His cheesy accent sounded even cheesier in my headset. I shook my head and returned the grin. It was a strange feeling having someone next to me again as you dove into the maw of the enemy. It was different, but not unwanted. Maybe I would come out of it in one piece. And then again, maybe it would all be left to a flip of fate's coin.

THE CLICKS of Natasha's heels echoed in the dim corridor. She left the arriving guests to Joe's men, the ones who would escort the VIPs to the parade ground and the elegant tables the caterer had arranged earlier. The wine was chilled and the bar well-stocked. They would not need waiters or chefs. Everything was ready.

Natasha wrapped the sable coat tight around her body. Her evening dress did little to fend off the creeping cold and the subtle dampness of the fort's tunnels.

When she arrived at the thick cell door, Natasha ordered the lone guard to unlock it. He complied and stepped aside.

Someone had left a sputtering butane lamp in the corner. Its dancing flames illuminated the figure sitting against the far wall. Ed Walker's face looked up as she entered, his eyes cold and steady.

"You look like shit, Eddie."

He didn't answer.

"I came to ask you to wish me luck."

Still no answer from her ex-husband.

"Oh, come on, Eddie. I won fair and square."

"This isn't a game, Natasha," he growled, shifting his handcuffed wrists in his lap.

Natasha shrugged. It was all a game.

"We could've been something, Eddie."

He shook his head and looked away.

"You don't deserve me," he said. This time his voice was strained.

Natasha laughed. How things had changed. She really had loved him, even after he'd left with Anna. It was the treasure of first love. The first years had been tough. Time made it easier, and yet, there were days she still longed for his touch. Strange. Another weakness.

She stared at him, remembering the good times they'd had, sighing at the memories.

"Well, it's time to go," she said, moving closer, smelling the sweat and tart body odor seeping from her ex. His hands and feet were cuffed and shackled to one another. She made sure of that with a tug, eliciting a wince from the fallen pastor. Natasha bent down and looked into his eyes. "Good night, Eddie." She leaned in and kissed him on the lips. He did not pull away.

"Ms. Varushkin," the guard interrupted, "Joe says the last of the guests have arrived."

Natasha slipped back from her former lover, and gave him a pat on the cheek.

"I have to go," she said, receiving no reply from the condemned man. She smiled sadly and turned to leave.

The guard locked the door, but before he could go back to his boring post, he felt a hand on his forehead and then something cold on his neck. The blade bit and his body stiffened. One hand went for the blade and the other tried to grab whoever was behind him. It was too late.

With experience born of practice, Natasha's cut was deep and perfect. By the time she'd grabbed the pistol from the man's holster and tossed it down the corridor, the man was gurgling blood and writhing on the ground like a beached fish.

Careful to avoid the spurting blood, Natasha grabbed the keys from where the guard had dropped them on the floor, and unlocked the cell door. She pulled it open three inches and left it and the keys where they were.

Happy with her handiwork, the heir to the Varushkin fortune looked around one last time and headed to her dinner party. She was, after all, host of the momentous event.

CHAPTER THIRTY-THREE

"**O**ne minute," the pilot said over the headset.

Rex and I each gave him a thumbs-up. The next part would be a little tricky. Instead of jumping out of the side doors, we were going to use the ingenious upgrade under our feet. Once the seats were folded back, there was a button in the cockpit that triggered a hydraulic ramp which served as the bottom of the aircraft. Once fully opened, we would ease our way into the opening and drop. That was the theory at least.

The only drops I'd ever made were out of big cargo planes made for dropping parachutists out the back. I imagined getting sucked out of the bottom of the aircraft when the pilot pressed the button. That didn't happen.

First the red light next to my head flickered on, signaling that the ramp was about to open. It struggled against the air current, the plane's aerodynamic stream suddenly changing. When it was all the way open, Rex grinned and pointed. He was waiting for me to go first.

I looked at the opening dubiously, wondering if I could get my frame and the chute through the space. The last thing

I needed was to get caught on something and be left dangling out into nothingness.

As the old military saying goes, *slow is smooth and smooth is fast*. I eased my way into the hole, propping my weight on my forearm. The buffeting wind caught my legs and I counted to three in my head. As I pushed myself off like a diver going down a port hole, I felt a dreaded snag, but a split second later, it was gone.

I flipped around and got my bearing, the compass and GPS mounted on my wrist already calculating my arrival. A couple seconds later, I heard three clicks in my earpiece. Rex was safely away.

We fell toward Georges Island, silent as diving cranes. With any luck, we'd step onto Ft. Warren with a measure of the same stealth.

"DROP CONFIRMED," Julian Fog heard over the radio. He was twenty feet under water, the dark Boston Harbor obscuring his view as he swam point, three volunteers behind him. Fog focused on his own compass, pushing away the feeling he always got when diving at night. It was like swimming through ink. You could see your compass and not much else. If you didn't trust your equipment, it was easy to get turned around and even swim straight to the bottom. Night diving was all about monitoring your depth, calculating your course and distance, and controlling your breathing.

They were going up against a superior force, but Fog had every confidence in his men. Daniel and Rex could handle themselves. Hell, Snake Eyes was a one man army. During his time in the fleet, Fog had been privy to most of Sgt. Briggs's operations. The Marine had seen more than most and had somehow come out unscathed each and every time. There had been a running joke in the battalion at the time. Got a fucked up op that only Rambo can handle? Dial in Snake Eyes. Only thing was, it wasn't a joke. Daniel went about his job with quiet efficiency. He never made waves and never complained.

As he shifted his course a bit to the east, Fog wondered if the former sniper was still every bit as lethal as he had been.

———

NATASHA VARUSHKIN STOOD at the head of the lavish table. All eyes watched as she raised a glass of chardonnay.

"To The Pension," she began. "May it be the beginning of something extraordinary for our people."

There was a murmur of assent from her guests. Nineteen in all, they'd come from up and down the eastern seaboard. They were all over sixty-years-old, men of might and industry. They'd met over the last half century, mentored like her father as they rose through the ranks of the Soviet and Russian military, up the ladders of Russian corporations, and down the slippery slopes of government service.

What these men represented was not only the future of Russia, but its past as well. Like a living time capsule, these men had been trusted by others to plant the seed for the future. And what a seed they now grew. Not only were billions of dollars waiting in bank accounts across the globe, there were also the untold contacts these men had cultivated over their esteemed careers.

Some she had just met and others she knew through her father. They were secretive men, used to trusting no one as they lived their double lives. How they'd all arrived in America, she did not know. The important thing was that they were here now. It was her job to persuade them to take the next step.

"My father sends his best wishes," she continued, still standing as she looked up and down each side of the table. There was doubt in some eyes. Others masked their feelings and just stared with what she saw as mild interest. She would get their attention soon.

"Where is Georgy?" a man at the opposite end of the gathering asked.

"The injuries and infections my father endured during his imprisonment have led to certain complications. He is under twenty-four-hour watch by a team of physicians and promises to see you all soon." She heard grumbles from a few feet away but ignored them. "Now, I would like to tell you about the current state of The Pension, and what our combined assets will soon accomplish."

CHAPTER THIRTY-FOUR

As planned, I pulled my main chute at 3,000 feet. I waited for the telltale yank behind me, already bracing for it, but I felt nothing. Warning bells went off in my head as I went through the emergency routine, my body still falling at 115 miles per hour.

The next pull elicited a response, but not the one I wanted. I felt something flapping against the back of my head. My partially deployed chute inched out as I fell closer to the earth.

At 2,000 feet I ditched my main chute. The breakaway was clean and I kept falling. I could hear Rex's voice in my ear, but I couldn't answer as I struggled to deploy my reserve chute. It felt like it was caught. 1,500 feet. I yanked again. Still nothing.

920 feet, my altimeter said helpfully. I imagined it mocking me.

Finally, as I passed 750 feet, the ring moved, and my reserve chute deployed. This time I did feel the familiar tug from behind, and then I was slowing. I could now see the fort clearly, the lights from the festivities not far away. I took in a deep breath and glanced at my altimeter again. 300 feet. *Fuck*, I thought, reaching up to cue the radio and let Rex know I wasn't dead. My hand never got there.

All of a sudden, my left shoulder dipped and I heard a flutter overhead. What started as a left hand turn, soon turned into violent spinning. I tried to right my descent, but I got zero response from my handles.

180 feet.

The spinning got faster and I couldn't see my altimeter through my blurring vision. I was either going to be thrown or slammed. Neither option sounded promising. Instead of taking the ride down with the chute, I pulled my release, and hurtled down toward the coastline.

———

THE TWO GUARDS stopped at the sound of the splash. "What the hell was that?" the first one said, pulling out his oversized flashlight and shining it off the southern point of Georges Island.

"I better radio it in," said the second guard, already reaching for his mike.

"Hold on. Joe will have our ass if it's just a fish."

"That would've been one huge goddamn fish."

"Maybe a shark or dolphin then," said the first man, scanning the water. Then, as if in answer, something floated into view just outside the high-power beam. The two men stared as they walked closer. It looked like a ghost settled in over the water.

"Is that a—?"

Guard number two never got the rest of the question out. A burst of silenced rounds hit him in the back of the head. The first guard dropped the flashlight and did his best dive to the right. The rounds followed his rolling form, caught him in the leg and traveled up to his neck. His evasion was over.

REX FLARED his chute and executed a textbook landing, touching down right between the two fallen guards. After checking to make sure the men he'd shot were dead, he stowed the used chute and radioed for Daniel.

No answer.

He hadn't seen the sniper since he'd fallen from the plane, but he had caught the tail end of the conversation between the guards. Daniel had gone into the water.

Rex crept his way down to the water, his night vision goggles scanning the lapping harbor. Nothing.

Rex waded into the water up to his waist, still searching. No sound. No sign of Daniel.

"Echo Three, this is Six. Snake Eyes is down. I repeat, Snake Eyes is down."

NATASHA HAD ALREADY PINPOINTED the men who were going to be the problems. They sat with their arms crossed, refusing to touch their food or their drinks, like a coordinated hunger strike.

So as she described the thousand acre ranch in Wyoming, and the multitude of ventures their seed money had already purchased, she eyed the male chauvinists with amusement.

"I can see that some of you would still rather hear this from my father. Believe me when I tell you that I would like the same. But as the old American saying goes, the show must go on."

A former Russian general sitting halfway down the table

whispered to the man sitting next to him. His friend laughed. Natasha continued to ignore them.

"Now, for a little house cleaning." Heads swiveled back to the head of the table. "As most of you know, when my father first established the group that was to become The Pension, it was deemed necessary to cultivate certain...relationships within the underground communities. These relationships not only allowed some of you to come to America, they also assisted those of us smuggling in goods and currency that were used as a down payment for our initial investments. As time passed, my father wished to legitimize the inner workings of The Pension, and he put in place a plan to remove our organization from ever having to use our less than legal contacts ever again."

Natasha saw Joe prowling along the edge of the tent, trying to look unobtrusive and professional in his security uniform. She knew he was listening to her every word.

"I would like to announce that as of tonight, The Pension will no longer find it necessary to utilize these illegal contacts. As of tonight, The Pension is no longer bound by the rules that kept us shackled to the shadows for so many years. Tonight, our dream is realized."

There was polite clapping from most of the table. As she'd expected, Joe was making his way around the table and was soon standing just behind her.

"May I have a word?" he whispered.

Natasha turned as if she'd just realized he was there.

"I'm sorry, Joe. I meant to introduce you."

Joe's eyes narrowed. They moved from Natasha to the men at the table. She could see the indecision stamped on his face. Her comments about ceasing all illegal activity had struck a nerve. She'd promised him a merger. Joe needed to be seen as a man of power to men like those sitting at the table. Despite his growing influence, Joe was just another thug. He'd worked hard to make it to where he now reigned, but his vanity was an easy trigger to pull.

"Gentlemen, this is Joe. He is the current leader of one of the underground operations I just mentioned. Joe's business includes human trafficking and bribery. His friends are some of the very men who imprisoned my father and killed your friends."

Joe's face flushed.

"How dare you—"

The automatic weapon in Joe's hands rose until the front sight post was inches from Natasha's face. Natasha raised her hands over her head.

"If I misspoke, I am sorry, Joe. If you'd like to tell these men anything I missed—"

"Shut up, bitch."

"Are you going to shoot me now, Joe?"

The guests looked on, unperturbed by the disturbance. No doubt some of them hoped the man would pull the trigger. Natasha smiled as Joe tried to make a decision.

"If you're going to shoot me, do you mind if I put on some lipstick first?"

Joe's lips thinned and Natasha pointed to the table. There was a black Chanel tube laying next to her silverware.

Joe didn't move to stop her, so Natasha lowered her hands slowly and reached for the lipstick. After twisting off the top and extending the blood red wax, she touched it to her lips.

"Did you like the uniforms, Joe?" she asked.

The mobster's mouth twisted in a sneer. "I told you to shut up."

"I was just curious. I had them custom-made, you know. How about the hats? Do you like the hats?"

"What the fuck are you talking about?"

"The hats. They're the most important part."

"Step over there," Joe said, motioning outside the tent.

Apparently he didn't want her brains to splatter all over the distinguished guests. How thoughtful.

"I think I'll stay right here," Natasha said, even applying the deep red lipstick as his weapon pointed straight at her face.

"Fine. Now say goodbye to your father's friends," Joe said, lowering his head to the weapon, as if he really needed to take aim from the short distance.

Natasha chuckled.

"I think it's time for you to say goodbye, Joe. Your services are no longer needed."

Just as Joe's eyebrows scrunched in confusion, Natasha depressed the end of the lipstick tube, sending a radio signal to the fifteen receivers scattered around the island. The tiny receivers then sent an electric current into the thin explosive halos hidden inside the lining of each of the fifteen ball caps. The explosions were small compared to what one might see in a military demonstration, but they were plenty powerful enough to take off the tops of the heads of fifteen men disguised as private security guards.

The top half of Joe's skull was severed before he ever knew what happened. So localized was the detonation, that no blood reached the table. A thin line of it did hit Natasha's upraised hand, but she wiped it away with a napkin.

She took a seat, gazing down the table at the stunned expressions. Now they would listen.

"As I was saying, gentlemen, tonight is only the beginning. For your safety, my personal security detachment will soon arrive to ensure your well-being. Until then, why don't we begin the process of transferring your investments into The Pension's bank accounts."

Natasha pulled a laptop from under the table and logged into her secure back office.

Rex didn't see where the explosions had come from. They'd almost sounded like fireworks. Maybe the Russians were celebrating. With Daniel gone, it was up to him to get eyes-on. Fog and his men had just hit the northern shoreline, and they would be ready to scale the fort's walls soon. Rex had to push away all thoughts of his lost comrade and complete the mission. There would be time to mourn his passing later.

CIA operative Julian Fog didn't know what he was looking at. He could see the two forms on the ground, but they were obscured behind some scrub brush. Fog motioned for his men to fan out. When he got to the two bodies, he couldn't believe what he was seeing. Lying on the ground, one half on top of the other, were two men in security uniforms with the tops of their heads gone. It didn't make any sense.

Fog radioed Rex. "We've got two tangos down on the north end. Dark security uniforms. Both skulls are gone above the forehead."

It took a second for Rex to respond. When he did he sounded winded, like he was running. "Are you sure?"

"You think I'd make something like that up?"

"Okay. Maybe there's more bad guys we don't know about. I'm almost to where I can see the parade ground."

"We'll make our way to you."

"Roger. I'll let you know what I see."

Fog took one last look at the dead men on the ground and then motioned toward the grass topped stone wall looming up ahead, where the old gun emplacements were. Something told him this was just the beginning of an interesting night.

A DARK MASS emerged from the shallows, its form hunched and moving with no apparent haste. When it finally slipped out of the water and onto the sandy beach, the thing turned to the right and then to the left. Something inside its head knew it should move toward the large mass to the right, but its keen hearing caught the sound of something man-made to the left.

A motor, its predator mind registered. On instinct, the thing broke into a run, its legs tireless, its lungs fully expanded, its primitive mind yearning for blood.

CHAPTER THIRTY-FIVE

The forty-two-foot Boston Whaler 420 Outrage approached the Georges Island dock at low speed. Someone had failed to turn on the lights on the dock, and the only lights the boat had were the ones on the console. Duane Morosov was not amused. He called to the man in the bow.

"I'll need you to spot for me. I can't see shit."

"Neither can I," replied the man. His submachine gun was strapped over his shoulders. If everything was going according to plan on the island, the three men on the boat wouldn't need to use the weapons. They'd been handpicked by The Duchess. They knew all about the revised plan, about the attack against Joe's men, and had no qualms about following Natasha's lead. She'd given them their livelihoods in her father's absence, and they would not forget it.

The man in the bow said, "Twenty feet."

The coxswain threw the props in reverse for a second and then cut the engine.

"Man the lines," Morosov said, shouldering his own weapon and moving to join the guy up front.

The boat thumped against the dock and the man with the

bow line jumped out. After he secured the front of the vessel, Morosov stepped out and called for the guy in the back to throw him one of the stern lines. A line appeared out the darkness and almost slapped him in the face. He cursed as he snatched it from the air and bent over to secure his end to the dock.

"Will you turn on the lights?" he asked the guy on the dock, annoyed that he had to work in the near pitch-black.

His request was answered by a splash near the front of the boat.

"Sammy, you okay?" he asked.

No answer.

He secured the last fender and moved to find the idiot who'd fallen in the water.

"Sammy, what the fuck are you doing?"

There was nothing in the water except tiny swells knocking up against the boat.

"Sammy," he whispered this time. Maybe the jackass had knocked himself out. Natasha would be pissed, but he wasn't about to jump into the cold water and try to find the guy. Instead he went to find his second companion. "Miles, I think Sammy fell in the water."

There was a grunt from the stern. He lifted his weapon and said, "Miles? You okay?"

No answer.

Prickles spiked along his spine. He felt his finger move to the automatic weapon's trigger as he moved to where he'd heard the grunt.

"Miles, stop fucking around," Morosov hissed. Miles was the joker of the crew. He'd even done a stint as a stand-up comedian. That ended when his hobby could no longer pay the bills.

Now he could see the outline of Miles's large frame. He was sitting on the very back of the boat, his face facing astern like a kid deciding whether he wanted to jump in.

"Miles, what the…"

His words stuck in his throat. Miles wasn't sitting up. He was propped up by some kind of long wooden spear, the kind with the metal tip that they use on fishing boats, and it was sticking through the front of Miles's throat and poking out the back of his neck at a downward angle.

"Fuck," the last remaining crewman breathed, backing away from the swaying body. He bumped into something solid, realizing too late that he was still too far from the console to be touching it. When he whipped around, his weapon was stripped from his hands and he looked up at the leering face in the darkness. The eyes studied him as if the shrouded humanoid was deciding what to do.

Without warning, a hand clamped over Morosov's mouth, and he felt himself moving. The thing was on top of him as they flew into the air and then splashed into the water. The frigid cold blasted what air he had left in his lungs, and he did his best to fight off his attacker.

Two minutes later, Morosov's body drifted away from the dock, the dark shadow already heading inland.

———

REX APPROACHED the main entrance cautiously, sticking close to the thick walls. He didn't see anyone guarding the gatehouse. That was strange.

When he reached the gatehouse, Rex saw the first body. Just like Fog had described earlier, this one had the top of its skull removed. Rex gripped his weapon tighter and swept the area with his night vision. No more bodies that he could see.

As he slipped through the entryway, he didn't see the dark mass passing close behind. Instead of following Rex, the skulking form chose another way. It entered the fort's tunnel system.

———

THE CELL DOOR creaked open a few inches, and Pastor Walker looked up.

"Hello?" he said.

Silence answered him.

"Is anyone there?" he tried again.

Still no answer.

As he went to lay his head on his knees again, something blocked the meager light in the doorway.

"Who's there?"

Something dark and menacing shifted forward. Pastor Walker smelled something like damp earth and stale salt water. The shape moved closer. When it did, Walker caught what he thought was a hint of blond hair, obscured by something like a hood. When the form was close enough to touch, it bent down and Walker saw the eyes.

They were different somehow, but unmistakable.

"Daniel?"

The form nodded without saying a word and reached out to feel how the pastor was secured.

———

MY MIND SNAPPED BACK to the present, the beast pushed away for the moment, as my hands touched the pastor's restraints. The beast hadn't been surprised to find the door open, and in my awakening I wondered if maybe Rex or Fog had killed the guard outside the cell, and told Walker to stay put. I had no way of knowing since I'd lost my earpiece during my fall into the harbor.

My answer came a moment later as Walker stood up in one swift movement, the shackles clattering to the ground, a pistol with a silencer attached held in steady hands.

"Where is Anna?" Walker asked, his once-quivering face now relaxed, his tone even.

"You were in on it." My voice came out in a croak.

"Where is Anna?" he asked again, now moving around to put space between us.

"Fuck you," I said, my mind searching for the clues that I'd missed, the crumbs that had gone unnoticed.

Walker smiled.

"You really fell for it, didn't you? The poor bumbling pastor. I'll bet you never imagined I could pull this off."

This was a different man. I realized what he was, a chameleon. He was good. I'd give him that. To put on an act for so long. To bait me at every turn. I wondered how long he'd had me on the line.

"When?"

"When what?"

"When did you start tracking me?" I asked.

"I've got some locals who owe me some favors. One of them is that girl on the Pier, the one with the French Canadian friends."

"So you waited for someone like me to come along and then what?"

Walker shrugged.

"You military guys are all the same. Never back down from a fight. The ones that didn't get the shit kicked out of them were offered a place to stay."

"Let me guess, at your farm?"

"No. You were the first to stay there. We kept the others in neutral territory until it was time to move them," he said, the gun still pointed at my chest.

"What did you do with them?"

He rolled his eyes like he didn't have time to explain everything. Then he changed his mind. "They were put in the pipeline. Our clients have unusual tastes."

"So you sold them."

"Of course."

My stomach turned.

"And then you came along. The way you dispatched the morons at the bar made us realize you were special. When you found the shelter and I let you disarm me, I knew we'd found our man."

I thought back to that day, to how angry I'd been, and how disgusted he'd made me by his confession. My temper had helped mask his ruse. I'd fallen right into his trap and ended up doing all the dirty work for him.

"And Anna?" I asked.

"What about Anna?"

"Did she know? Is she part of this?"

"Of course not," he said, like the idea was preposterous. I wondered if he realized how twisted it sounded coming out of his mouth.

"And what was there to gain? You manipulated me into—"

His laugh cut me off.

"I didn't have to manipulate you. You did it all on your own. All we had to do was present the problem, and you did the rest."

He was right. I'd done it all willingly. He'd dangled the carrot and I hopped right after it.

"I really wish I could've been there for the whole thing. What you did to Adam Eplar, the guy at the car wash? Masterful! The way you plugged those pricks at the brownstone? Classic! But what really made me respect you, what really made me realize we'd stumbled onto something special, was when you called in your buddies. Not only did the FBI play a key role in taking out our enemies, they even brought in the CIA to help. Man, I can't tell you how grateful I am that you stepped off of that train."

Anger and confusion coursed through me like a toxic mix of lethal drugs. For the first time I could remember, I couldn't move. Even the beast in me cowered in a corner, covering its face with one massive paw. *You are broken.*

I'd missed part of what Walker was saying. He was really enjoying his new role as master of intrigue. I listened half-heartedly as he bragged on.

"Now that Joe's gone and we have the managing members of The Pension in hand, I'm sure the CIA would love to make a deal with us. They have a long history of going with the winning team."

My eyes cleared and I heard a loud gong go off in my head, like a call to quarters. I was broken, but at least I knew it now. Something told me that even though I was broken I could be fixed. *You are not lost*, the voice said.

My body relaxed. The beast growled. Walker went on talking.

"So what do you say? You help me put this deal together and I'll see if I can convince Natasha to give you a pass."

"And what about her father?"

"He'll have to go, of course. Natasha's setting the groundwork for that now."

"And you'll let me go if I help you?"

"I'll do my best."

I nodded. "I'll do it."

He only looked surprised for a split second. When he motioned for me to lead the way out the door, his face was full of confidence, the conquering hero for his beloved Natasha.

"One last question," I said, turning to look over my shoulder. He was a comfortable distance behind, knowing exactly how far a normal man would need to counterattack.

"What?"

"What happens to Anna?"

Walker shrugged.

"She'll come around. Once she understands that the real world isn't all rainbows and lollipops, Anna will become part of what we've built. I did this for Anna *and* for Natasha. This way I get my family back and a comfortable life to go with it. Don't worry about Anna. She'll figure it out. Kids always do when you're honest with them. "

I nodded and turned back to the door, taking sure steps to the exit.

No normal man could've attacked from that distance. But I was no normal man. With the flick of a switch, I unchained the beast.

———

AT FIRST, Walker thought Daniel had tripped. Just to be safe, he took a step back. But as he watched, the dark mass sprang away from him and toward the wall. With a speed that left his mouth hanging open, Daniel rebounded off the wall and flew over the impossible distance between them. He'd twisted in the air, and Walker's eyes went wide and met the dilated pupils of a monster. His hesitation cost him his readiness and then his gun. The collision with the stone floor blasted the air from his lungs.

Like a Western gunslinger, Daniel whipped the pistol around in his hand and snarled. The barrel of the weapon was pointed in the other direction. Walker thought that maybe Daniel wouldn't shoot him. That shred of hope lasted a second longer until the butt of the pistol slammed down on Walker's nose.

The beast did not stop until Walker's face was a bloody pulp, and the pastor was well on his way to his final judgment.

CHAPTER THIRTY-SIX

R ex Hazard and Julian Fog's team watched as Natasha Varushkin called each man up to the laptop to complete their transactions. Video and audio were being relayed back to their makeshift headquarters where Georgy Varushkin was witnessing his daughter's betrayal.

Two-thirds of the table was done when something diverted Natasha's attention.

Rex looked to the right and saw a dark figure dragging something out into the huge courtyard.

"Can you see who that is?" Rex asked Fog over the radio.

"Negative."

———

NATASHA FINISHED THE LATEST TRANSFER, and excused herself from the table. She'd seen the figure emerging from the old cell block, and walked that way.

He'd done it faster than she'd thought. Ed said this Daniel would probably try to save the day. Eddie thought that the drifter was some kind of war hero. When she'd given him the keys to the handcuffs and slipped the pistol into his lap, she'd made him promise to do it quickly. He'd smiled. Eddie had always been a show off. It had been his idea to go to seminary and become a pastor. He said it was fun pretending in front of all those hypocrites. Whenever they got together for secret liaisons, he bragged about how the parishioners loved him, and how this and that pastor would call and ask how he was doing such and such things.

Now there he was, her Eddie. She recognized his clothes now. He was dragging something. It must have been heavy because he was walking backwards, straining to pull the load.

"Eddie," she said, now twenty feet from her soon-to-be second-time-husband.

He just grunted like it was all he could do to pull the thing along the ground. It was a body. Why was he bringing the body? She could see that the face was smashed and bloody. What had he done?

"Eddie," she said as she reached out to touch his shoulder. "Why did you—"

Eddie pivoted and grabbed her by the throat. She tried to claw the hand off, but it wouldn't budge. Her eyes bulged as she saw the stranger's eyes. They locked onto hers and refused to let go.

"Eddie's gone," the man said in a raspy voice.

The edges of her vision blurred. She tried to cry. She tried to scream. She tried to fall.

The man held her up, his grip tightening, his eyes uncaring, unrelenting. *Daniel*, she thought.

"And now you die," she heard him say, his voice far off like in a dream. Then, as the pain intensified and her field of vision collapsed, the world closed in and swallowed her.

EPILOGUE

I don't know who took care of the cleanup. Probably Rex or maybe even Julian Fog.

By the time we got back to the mainland, my body and mind were on the verge of collapse. I don't remember anything after crashing onto the bed.

REX SAID I slept for twenty-four hours. I believed him. While my mind still moved like sludge, my body had somehow gotten away unscathed. I'd fallen from who knew how many feet in the air, and somehow I was still alive. It wasn't the first time something like that had happened, but I wasn't about to think about why it had happened. I knew it was better not to think.

Why did some people come home from war and some didn't?

That was the kind of question I didn't like to ask.

Georgy, carried by the ever-present Vasily, was my second visitor.

After we'd talked about what he was doing to repair the

damage Natasha had done (he never mentioned my role in her death, even though I was sure he knew), he brought up Anna.

"Anna does not know the truth of what happened," he said.

I nodded, but didn't say anything.

"I'm sure you understand what such knowledge could do to a young girl."

I nodded again.

"I will not ask you to lie, Daniel, but I will ask you to choose your words wisely. In one day's time, Anna lost her mother and her father. I would just ask that you consider her emotional well-being when you speak to her."

"I understand," I said, even though I had no idea what I was going to say to her.

"Good. Now, I wanted to thank you for all that you have done for my family."

Jesus. I'd just killed his only daughter and he was thanking me?

He went on. "I am a man with a long memory. I hope that you will consider yourself as I do, as I'm sure Anna considers you, to be part of our family. If there is anything you ever need, money, a place to stay, call me. Your friends Rex and Julian will know how to find me."

"Thanks," I said, not really feeling that I deserved his gratitude.

———

THE NEXT TIME I WOKE, Anna was sitting on the corner of the bed. Her eyes were swollen and she held a tissue in her hand.

"How long have you been sitting there?" I asked.

"Not long," she sniffed.

"How are you feeling?"

"Crappy."

I wanted her to say something, to ask me one of her millions of questions. Instead she sat there, staring at me.

For the first time in ages, I opened my heart. *God, please take care of her. She didn't deserve this.* I didn't know if my plea would help, but I hoped it would.

"Poppa said you'd tell me how my dad died."

Did she know? Was she just testing me? Shit.

"Nobody told you?" I asked.

Anna shook her head.

I let out a long exhale and said, "He died saving my life."

I held her gaze until she nodded.

"Thank you," she said, a glimmer of the Anna I first met in her ice blue eyes.

"No, Anna, thank you," I said. In those four words was my hope for the future. She'd given me a glimpse into true love, into what gleeful joy really looked like. When I'd met her, Anna lived in a world with no barriers, where anyone with a dream could achieve it as long as they were curious and kind. I hoped with all my heart that she would find that peace again.

———

REX AND FOG drove me to the train station. Along the way, Fog told me about how certain agency pricks were trying to step in and take control of The Pension operation.

"Over my dead body," Fog said. He would be the link between Georgy Varushkin and the CIA. He was a perfect fit. Fog would keep Georgy's secret and Georgy would provide Fog with whatever intelligence he could gather. "You know he'd give you anything you want, right?" he asked me. "He said the rest of the managing members voted on setting aside an unnamed amount of money in your name, just in case you wanted to come in out of the cold."

"I don't need it," I said.

"The hell you don't," Rex laughed. "Who wouldn't want a paid-for retirement plan just waiting for them?"

"Don't dismiss it," Fog said seriously. "It's really nice of them to do it."

"I know," I said, meaning it. But I didn't want the money. I had everything I needed, or so I thought.

When I stepped out of the car at the station, Rex offered his hand and said, "Hey, don't be a stranger, okay?"

"I'll try," I said honestly.

He nodded and rolled up the window.

I MADE one more stop before heading in to buy my ticket west. The guy at the tiny liquor store didn't want to break the hundred-dollar bill I gave him. He looked me up and down like I was a counterfeiter. Finally, he handed over the brown paper sack and my change.

When I got to the ticket booth, I looked up at the schedule. Ontario, Canada, at 9:30am. Then my eyes moved down the line. For some reason Seattle, Washington, leaving at 10:15am caught my attention.

"Can I help you, sir?" asked the swarthy woman behind the ticket counter.

"Do you have a quarter?" I asked.

"You don't have any money?"

I pulled out a couple hundreds and laid them on the counter.

"Can I borrow a quarter?" I asked again.

With the reluctance of a public servant, she opened the register and handed me a quarter. I turned it over in my hand. Heads or tails?

I flicked the quarter off of my thumb and into the air. It got level with the counter before I snatched it out of the air with my left hand and slapped it onto the back of my right. I looked down and smiled.

"One ticket to Seattle, please."

———

I hope you enjoyed this story.
If you did, please take a moment to write a review on AMAZON. Even the short ones help!

GET A FREE COPY OF THE CORPS JUSTICE PREQUEL SHORT STORY, *GOD-SPEED*, JUST FOR SUBSCRIBING AT CG-COOPER.COM

ALSO BY C. G. COOPER

The Corps Justice Series In Order:

Back To War

Council Of Patriots

Prime Asset

Presidential Shift

National Burden

Lethal Misconduct

Moral Imperative

Disavowed

Chain Of Command

Papal Justice

The Zimmer Doctrine

Sabotage

Liberty Down

Sins Of The Father

Corps Justice Short Stories:

Chosen

God-Speed

Running

The Daniel Briggs Novels:

Adrift

Fallen

Broken

Tested

The Tom Greer Novels

A Life Worth Taking

The Spy In Residence Novels

What Lies Hidden

The Alex Knight Novels:

Breakout

The Stars & Spies Series:

Backdrop

The Patriot Protocol Series:

The Patriot Protocol

The Chronicles of Benjamin Dragon:

Benjamin Dragon – Awakening

Benjamin Dragon – Legacy

Benjamin Dragon - Genesis

ABOUT THE AUTHOR

C. G. Cooper is the USA TODAY and AMAZON
BESTSELLING author of the CORPS JUSTICE novels
(including spinoffs), The Chronicles of Benjamin Dragon and
the Patriot Protocol series.

Cooper grew up in a Navy family and traveled from one
Naval base to another as he fed his love of books and a
fledgling desire to write.

Upon graduating from the University of Virginia with a
degree in Foreign Affairs, Cooper was commissioned in the

United States Marine Corps and went on to serve six years as an infantry officer. C. G. Cooper's final Marine duty station was in Nashville, Tennessee, where he fell in love with the laid-back lifestyle of Music City.

His first published novel, BACK TO WAR, came out of a need to link back to his time in the Marine Corps. That novel, written as a side project, spawned many follow-on novels, several exciting spinoffs, and catapulted Cooper's career.

Cooper lives just south of Nashville with his wife, three children, and their German shorthaired pointer, Liberty, who's become a popular character in the Corps Justice novels.

When he's not writing or hosting his podcast, Books In 30, Cooper spends time with his family, does his best to improve his golf handicap, and loves to shed light on the ongoing fight of everyday heroes.

Cooper loves hearing from readers and responds to every email personally.

To connect with C. G. Cooper visit
www.cg-cooper.com

MORE THANKS TO MY BETA READERS:

Alex, Julie, Richard, Marsha, Kathy, John, Don H., Bob, Pat, Mary, Pam, Don D., Wanda, Susan, Glenda, Cheryl and David: Thank you, thank you, thank you. A million and one thanks.

56817082R00145

Made in the USA
Columbia, SC
01 May 2019